COLLIDE

A FLIPPIN' FANTASTIC ROMANCE

STEPHANIE SHEA

Copyright © 2021 by STEPHANIE SHEA

All rights reserved. No part of this publication may be reproduced, distributed, or transmitted in any form or by any means, or stored in a database or retrieval system, without written permission from the author, except in the case of brief quotations embodied in critical articles and reviews. To request permission and for all other inquiries, contact stephaniesheawrites@gmail.com.

This is a work of fiction. Names, characters, businesses, places, events and incidents are either the products of the author's imagination or used in a fictitious manner. Any resemblance to actual persons, living or dead, business establishments, events, or locales is purely coincidental.

Edited by Amanda Elle Edits

SYNOPSIS

Mia Stone isn't looking for romance. Not after her engagement crashed to an end when her fiancé was caught on viral video kissing another woman. She has time and space for three things in her life. Her family, her best friends Darby and James, and Flippin' Fantastic Renovations—the house flipping company they co-own.

Lauryn Matthews gets a bad rap. The women, the scandals... It's not her fault drama follows her everywhere. In fact, the instant fame thing gets to her more than anyone knows. Except maybe her therapist. All she wants is a place to call home, and all roads lead to Denver.

Mia and Lauryn collide at a local lesbian bar on New Year's Eve, and fireworks go off. The good, bad and the ugly. But when Lauryn turns out to be Mia's newest client, can they put aside their differences long enough to acknowledge the undercurrent of romance between them? Or will an unspoken grudge forever keep them at odds?

Collide is the second novella in a trio of Flippin' Fantastic romances about the three women who own and operate Flippin' Fantastic Renovations. Pencil in this slow burn lesfic romance for the perfect Valentine's Day read.

CHAPTER 1

Mia grabbed her scorecard and did a quick take around the floor for Darby and James. Ten dates in, less than halfway through the night and after the last round, the chances she would make it through Revel's New Year's Eve speed dating event were about…

Zero.

There were few things she hated more than disappointing Darby—she *had* gone through the trouble of dragging Mia and James here with the purest of intentions—but so far, Mia had been made to sit through one date with a woman who'd clearly downed one too many Mai Tais, another who had managed to sum up a lifetime of tragedy in four minutes and one who had pitched Mia what was decidedly a Ponzi scheme.

The woman on the opposite end of the small bar table slid back her chair, standing. "Are you sure we don't know each other?"

Mia nodded, repeating for the seventh time since they'd sat down, "I'm sure." She *was* sure. She hadn't gone to

Colorado College, or played in the local soccer league. She definitely was not the weather woman on Channel 2 or—

"I know!" The woman clapped her hands and grinned. "You worked at that sex shop on Broadway."

Mia's face scrunched up. "Um, no." She caught sight of James' red flannel in a cluster by the bar, offered her date a muttered, "Nice meeting you, bye," and was pushing through the crowd of mingling speed daters before the woman could think up another place where they had certainly not met.

The boom of an early 2000s hit—Mariah Carey's Heartbreaker?—blared through the speakers, red and purple flashes beaming all around the otherwise darkened lounge. The dates had been set up on the dancefloor, but whoever had coordinated this thing obviously didn't plan on giving themselves too much work between speed dating ending at ten and the New Year club crowd rolling in around eleven.

Halfway to the bar, a hand looped around hers and her head snapped right to find Darby next to her. "Oh my God, this was a terrible idea."

"Hate to say I told you so, babe."

"It seemed like fun in theory." Darby pouted, pushing her chocolate brown hair behind one ear then straightening her glasses. "All the cute women who love women you can date in one place. Like, *Her*...but without the risk that the girl you've been talking to for three months is a catfish."

Mia laughed. "Right."

"Plus, you and James were supposed to find love tonight."

"Uh huh." Mia was absolutely in love... with the idea of staying single. Probably forever.

"Do you think she's having fun?"

They paused as they got to the crowded bar, watching

James' failing and awkward attempts to create any amount of space between herself and the other women. Six-foot tall and adorably lanky, there was no missing her. "Yeah." Mia nodded. "Think she's having a blast, Darbs."

Darby turned to Mia. "Okay, but promise you'll help me convince her to stay for the second round. She could still meet someone. *You* could still meet someone."

It was just like Darby to find the bright side in every scenario—in fact, sometimes she *was* the bright side—but she was right. Surely, there was at least one woman in Revel tonight that each of them could connect with. At the very least, invite home and happily never see again. Mia wasn't looking for love, not after how her last relationship had ended, but maybe this night could still turn out to be some kind of fun.

"Thank all that is good in the universe."

Mia looked up to find James facing them with two drinks precariously clutched in one hand and a third in the other. Her hand shot up and claimed the apple martini. "Ugh. I love you." Drink on the edge of her lips, she paused, furrowing her brows. "These are for us, right, and not two other women you've won over with all that sexy James Dean charm?"

James rolled her eyes, passing the Shirley Temple to Darby. "Sure, M. Total lady killer over here."

"One minute, daters!" The host squealed over the music.

Mia groaned. How had it been five minutes already?

James passed an anxious gaze over the room. "Please tell me we're not staying."

Darby shot Mia a pleading look before squeezing James' arm. "We can do this. Just remember, beautiful women are people, too."

"You don't even have to say much," Mia added. She still wasn't completely onboard with Darby's latest stroke of genius, but she'd always be supportive of James getting past her fear of talking to women she found attractive. "Just flash those dimples and your southern drawl will do the rest."

"Twenty seconds!"

Around them, some of the daters had started shuffling toward the tables on the dancefloor. Mia, Darby and James followed reluctantly.

"I just want it on record that I am *not* having fun and if I have to increase the frequency of my therapy sessions, we're charging the company card," James muttered.

Darby wrapped her in a one-armed hug, "Good thoughts, J, good thoughts."

Good thoughts, Mia told herself.

So, it was settled.

The worst queer women in all of Denver had gathered at Revel tonight to remind Mia exactly why she would likely never date again. And now that she thought about it, it made complete sense. All the well-adjusted, delightfully eccentric women were either at home right now cuddled up with their partner, or out together having a lovely, preferably longer than four-minute date. Which left her with, counting the last two rounds only, the lady who had FaceTimed her mom just so Mia could be *introduced* to all seven of her cats and Tiger the turtle, and the one who kept complimenting her on how pretty she was. The latter at least had been a nice ego boost, but this...

Her current date sniffled, and Mia sighed, handing the woman another napkin. "It's just, she promised we would always be together, you know, and then she left me for a scuba diving pizza delivery woman?"

"That...is not a real thing."

"It is." The woman blew her nose. "At that underwater hotel in Florida."

Mia made a mental note to look that up. "Okay, well, I know it doesn't seem like it right now, but you're going to be okay." Darby had said something almost identical to Mia six months ago, or was it James who'd talked her off of that hill?

"I just don't understand."

"I know. Exes suck."

"They do!"

The bell dinged, signaling the end of the round and thankfully saving Mia from having to sit through another second of this torture. She reached out to pat her date's hand sympathetically then pulled back at the last minute. "It's her loss. Really."

Her brows—a radiant ginger—sloped above tearful green eyes. "You think so?"

"I know so." In the peripheral of her gaze, Mia caught sight of Darby rushing in her direction. "Nice date," she mumbled, scrambling to her feet just as Darby had crossed her table. "You okay, Darbs?"

"Mhm." Darby nodded quickly. "I just need to run to coat check and back."

"Coat check?"

"I left my inhaler in my pocket. Go see how James is doing? I think she just got the radio host. Pazecki something. And you know how she gets around the chatty ones."

Mia instinctively glanced across the room to where she'd last seen James, only to find that she'd already left her table. "She probably just went to the b—" Mia's brows furrowed as she turned to find the space where Darby had been standing empty.

Another 2000s hit boomed.

Her gaze went to the bar. The colored lights dancing around the room didn't do much for visibility, but she was pretty sure she knew the head of short messy hair sticking out among the rest. She'd probably only seen about three other women who were as tall as James tonight. It had to be James but... Mia furrowed her brows. Why would James be taking her shirt off?

She started toward the bar again, mumbling *excuse me* and *I'm sorry* nearly every other step. When she'd finally made it close enough, she locked in on James nervously adjusting her plain V-neck while the woman in front of her appeared to now be wearing James' flannel?

Mia's lips parted to ask before she quickly discarded the thought. She would definitely be questioning James about what kind of strange dating ritual she'd been talked into by a gorgeous stranger with very impressive breasts, but right now, they needed to find Darby. "We've got a code red." Mia took James by the elbow. "I need you."

MIA PUSHED OPEN the heavy metal door, tugging her coat on as she stepped into the brisk night air outside of Revel. She jerked to a stop at the sound of Darby's voice and James stumbled into her.

"Watch it, M," James murmured indignantly.

Darby and the bouncer they'd passed on their way in earlier both turned to look at Mia and James. "This must be the search party." The bouncer grinned, pulling a beanie over her black tapered haircut then stuffing both hands into the pockets of her windbreaker.

Darby laughed. "Hey, you two." The familiar buoyancy of her tone was welcomed, but nothing like she'd been when she'd rushed off earlier in search of her inhaler.

James leaned closer, whispering in Mia's ear, "I thought you called a code red."

"Well..." Mia's gaze shifted between Darby and the bouncer. "You okay, Darbs?" she asked again for good measure.

"Never better." Darby turned to the bouncer, her lips stretched in an open smile. "This is Astrid. I'm helping her move tomorrow."

"Of course you are. Hi, Astrid." Mia offered her hand for a quick shake.

James nodded at Astrid, "James," then turned to Darby. "Not to interrupt whatever y'all were up to out here in the freezing cold, but Mia promised we could leave once we found you. So, the only way anyone is getting me back in there is kicking and screaming."

Mia chuckled. "I think we can all agree that none of us want to go back in there."

Darby said a brief goodbye to Astrid then slid between Mia and James, linking arms with them much like she had earlier. "Okay, so this turned out to be not so fun. My offer's still on the table to make you both online dating profiles, though."

"First, let's just make it through New Year's Eve."

They started along the sidewalk toward the parking lot, recounting their terrible dates and comparing notes where they'd all dated the same women. Mia could safely say this was literally the only time that would ever happen. Darby and James may have been her best friends, but they were as opposite as it gets, and she wouldn't change a thing. Maybe they'd had a bad night out, but a part of her was glad Darby had dragged them to Revel tonight. She needed the distraction. She needed to not think about where she'd been this time last year and who she'd been with—walking through Observatory Park, taking low quality pictures with her—

"Shit." Mia stopped, their linked arms forcing Darby and James to come to a halt too.

"What's wrong?"

"My purse. I left it in the club," she explained

James rose a skeptical brow at her. "The one you still won't throw away from she-who-is-dead-to-us?"

"No." Mia scrunched up her face. "The one I bought after we sold the first house we flipped."

"Oh. Well, let's go get it," Darby offered.

Mia shook her head. "It's okay. I'll go. Get the car and meet me out front?"

"Yeah. Okay."

Mia turned in the opposite direction.

"Hey, M," James called, and Mia glanced back at her. "Still time for one last date. You just might find love yet."

"Remind me...what happened to your flannel again?" Mia teased.

James shot her a look and Darby just looked confused. "Wait, what *did* happen to your shirt?"

Mia smiled, shaking her head as she made her way toward Revel. There was no doubt in her mind that she would not run into love tonight.

CHAPTER 2

Lauryn stuffed her hands into the pockets of her quilted walker jacket and lowered her chin into the faux fur collar. Denver on New Year's Eve. Honestly, what was she thinking leaving perfectly warm LA for the fucking arctic? Probably that she didn't want to ring in another year getting too drunk on overpriced champagne then falling into bed with another model she had nothing in common with. Then again, would that have been so bad?

She gazed down at the light layer of snow dusting her boots and gently kicked at the pavement before glancing up at the three-story brick building in front of her.

Revel.

Maybe she was a bit bored with the revolving daydream of overnight fame she'd just woken to one morning. No. Bored wasn't right. Intimidated, maybe. More than that, she knew she wasn't running from LA so much as she'd run to the one place that could feel even remotely like going home. This time of year... Thanksgiving. Christmas. New Year. She still hadn't found the hack to handling it all without losing herself to too much thinking.

A brisk wind picked up around her and she clenched her arms closer to her body and started for the door. The air buzzed with that pre-countdown excitement so typical of a New Year's Eve. Laughter, yelled conversations, a gleeful scream from somewhere in the distance. A line spanned one half of the building and disappeared around the side. She narrowed her gaze at the bouncer, hoping it was someone she knew. The last thing she needed was a newbie dropping her name in front of two dozen people waiting to get inside a club, especially since she'd just gotten to that stage in her career where she was famous enough to be recognized, but too fresh to not be judged for declining to sign autographs and pose for pictures. And after the Instagram thing?

Lay low.

Those were her instructions. That's what she was doing.

It wasn't her fault her oldest friend just happened to manage a local hotspot. She stopped in front of the bouncer, smiling as she angled her body away from the line of people.

"Astrid."

The woman's face lit up with a grin. "Lo."

Lauryn tried to tune out the mumbles stirring up from the line. "Hey."

"Strange thing seeing you here on a big night like this. Thought you'd be on a stage in Times Square or something."

Lauryn chuckled. "Maybe next year." She signaled the line with a slight bob of her head. "Think they'll mob you if I just slip by?"

Astrid laughed. "I think we'll manage."

"Right. Happy New Year, Ash."

The second bouncer pulled the door open, unleashing a

blare of music, and Lauryn glanced over her shoulder to mumble a thanks when she collided with something else. A phone clattered to the floor and stopped by her boots. Half an inch away, an expensive-looking red wallet lay open with a few bills threatening to spill out. "Shit. Sorry." She quickly picked up the phone and wallet, taking the time to close it—was that presumptuous?—before looking up at the person in front of her. Her lips parted, "Uhm," and she stared—blatantly, helplessly stared—at the woman before catching herself. "Sorry," she mumbled again. "I think these belong to you." She might have handed the phone and wallet over slower than intended.

The woman smiled, her lips full in ways the word "full" didn't begin to do justice. Plump?

"It's fine. I think I could've been paying a little more attention." She accepted her phone, her fingers brushing against Lauryn's before she held it up. "Can't live without them, right?"

"Guess not." Lauryn laughed, reaching up to push the collar of her jacket down from her face and drop the hood from her head. She wasn't sure if it was because it was warmer inside, or because suddenly, maybe she wouldn't mind being recognized after all.

The woman's smile faded as she took a step back, and Lauryn's eyes inadvertently trailed her body from the gold buttons on her double-breasted wool coat to her exposed legs. She didn't seem very tall, but the ankle strap heels on her feet easily added five inches. She was going *outside*, in *that*?

"You've got to be fucking kidding me."

Lauryn met her eyes again. Darkest shade of brown, beguiling even in this lighting.

Jesus, Lo. Get a grip.

The woman started past her. "Right when I thought this night couldn't get any worse."

Lauryn blinked, catching her by the elbow then immediately dropping her hand to her side. "Excuse me?"

She scoffed, eying Lauryn from head to toe. "No, *Lauryn Matthews*. You're not fucking excused." She pushed past the bouncers and disappeared beyond the heavy metal door.

"What?" Lauryn furrowed her brows, half-entertaining the idea of going after this stranger that was decidedly not a fan. She stifled the impulse—the thud in her chest and rush in her veins; that thing, that feeling she didn't get often. She shrugged out of her jacket and went inside.

Lauryn kept her head down as she pushed her way through the crowded dancefloor in the direction of Sully's office. There was very little chance of her getting noticed with the poor visibility of strobe lights and she was grateful for only having to dodge one poorly aimed champagne spray on her way. The crowd seemed rowdy tonight, but that was to be expected.

The blue door at the end of the narrow hallway housing Sully's office was unmanned. Lauryn furrowed her brows, glancing over her shoulder as she stopped in front of it. She could grab her phone and shoot Sully a text, but on a night like this, ten to one chance Sully didn't even know where her own phone was. She brought a hand to the door, knocked and waited.

A remixed version of Taylor Swift's "New Year's Day" kicked up over the speakers. A little on the nose. The giggle of someone passing close by got caught in the hallway, and an image of that woman earlier surfaced in her mind. Her umber skin and terra cotta lips. What was it like? Her laugh. And what the hell did she have against Lauryn?

The door swung open. The look on Sully's face ran the gamut from frustrated to ecstatic in a single second. "Lo!"

"Surprise?"

Sully laughed, grabbing Lauryn's hand and pulling her in for a hug. "Get in here." She smelled exactly the same. Like sandalwood with the faintest signs of lime. One of those unique mixtures that lived deep in Lauryn's subconscious, locked away with all of her most precious memories until it was safe to uncover them. "I thought you wouldn't make it in until Monday." Sully pulled away and moved past Lauryn to shut the door behind them.

"Got an early meeting Monday, and I don't really feel like going straight off a plane." Lauryn went further into the office, eyes getting reacquainted with the dark tiles and silver-gray walls, one lined with framed mementos of Sully's favorite performances at Revel, some decades old, from days before the shift in ownership.

"Every time you walk in here, it's like you're checking to see if there's still room left on that wall."

"Maybe I am." Lauryn smiled, glancing down at the executive desk as she sank into one of two armchairs in front of it.

Sully slid into the leather high back chair behind the desk. Still keeping her office like a sixty-year-old mobster. "I'd put you up there now if you'd let me."

"Everyone on that wall earned their spot, Sul. I don't think it does me any favors if you just give me one because I'm your god daughter."

Sully's lips stretched in a subtle smirk, and then she shrugged. "Of course, it doesn't. Fix you a drink?"

Lauryn looked at her more keenly, searching for something in those kind emerald eyes and gracefully wrinkled face. The face of someone who had mothered and fathered her, been her best friend, too. And she hadn't said a word, but Sully knew what she was asking.

"Still sober." Sully beamed.

Lauryn leaned back into her chair with a relieved sigh. "I wasn't...*judging*, Sul. It's just—" This was probably the worst environment for a sober person, and she lived in constant fear Sully would slip. One drink. A line. It was for Sully's own good, but it was also selfish. Lauryn couldn't lose her.

Sully nodded. "I know, kiddo."

"No drink for me either, and before you say it, I know someone else drinking isn't going to send you on a bender. I mean, you did come back to this job."

"This about that party all over those tabloids then?"

Lauryn raised her brows. "You read the tabloids?"

"When your face is on the cover."

"You know that party was like six months ago, right? And I had nothing to do with the..."

"Drugs?"

"Yes." Lauryn folded her arms across her chest. She suddenly felt like she was being scolded by her mom—not that she'd ever really had one—and she'd already been through this with her publicist. Three times. "Why are you asking me about this now?"

"Why didn't you tell me about it when it happened?"

"Because it's embarrassing? Because I should know better? Because I didn't want to have to explain to *you*, of all people, Sul. I can't even begin to know what it's like for you, how hard you must fight every day, but I know I want to be someone who supports you, not—" Lauryn huffed. "Not whoever I was that night."

Sully stood and rounded her desk to sit in the armchair

next to Lauryn's. She rested her elbows on her knees and took Lauryn's hands in hers, the contrast between them like milk and honey. "You're a good kid, Lo. One mistake from half a year ago doesn't change that."

"You know I don't get the 'dumb kid' pass anymore at twenty-eight, right?"

Sully shrugged, grinning. "You get it from me. Mine should be the only opinion you're worried about."

"And maybe the five million other people who follow me on Instagram."

Sully shook her head. "Screw 'em."

Lauryn laughed. Denver on New Year's Eve. A dank manager's office in an overcrowded club. This was why she'd come. It was the only place that felt remotely like home.

"So, that woman," Sully said.

Lauryn furrowed her brows, glancing at the darkened monitor on Sully's desk. "You have cameras in the entrance way?"

"Of course, we have cameras in the entrance way. What does that have to do with it?"

"What do you—" Lauryn cut herself off. "Which woman?"

"The one on your lap in that picture." Sully narrowed her gaze. "Although, I am curious to know who you thought I meant."

Lauryn felt caught. Doing what, she didn't know. "That was no one."

"The one on your lap or in the entranceway?"

"The one on my la—Both."

Sully leaned back in her chair and smirked.

"I don't even remember her name." Lauryn frowned. And she didn't *know* her name—the woman she'd collided with earlier. She didn't know anything about her, except maybe that she had an affinity for designer clothes and most likely an intense skincare regime. And she didn't like Lauryn. That much was clear.

Beyond the walls of Sully's office, the countdown to midnight had begun—the chorus of voices faint but audible. In less than a minute, hordes of lovers would seal the end of one year and ring in a new with a kiss. With lust and love. And she didn't want to go to another Hollywood party tonight, get drunk and fall into bed with someone she barely knew. Yet here she was, reminiscent of the lips of a stranger.

CHAPTER 3

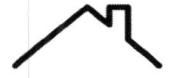

Mia was not having a Happy fucking New Year, and she was this close to telling the next person who casually shared their well wishes exactly that. Objectively, her morning hadn't been going that badly. Despite all the restlessness of the weekend, doing everything to keep herself busy, she'd woken this morning feeling pretty well rested. The weekend snowfall had dissipated, giving way to the sun, albeit silhouetted by a few stubborn clouds. But she was grateful for not having to trudge through six inches from her car to get to the office.

She didn't want to admit it, but New Year's Eve had left her in a hideous ditch of mood swings that she'd clawed her way out of months ago. After almost two hours of terrible dates. *Ugh.* Could she even call them that? In any case, she was more than happy to be out of there, happy to apologize to this stranger she'd run into, too. It was her fault. She hadn't been paying attention, too busy texting James and Darby that she was on her way out. And this stranger—dressed for a trip to the North Pole or something—had an endearing laugh and questionable fashion sense, but it was the nicest interaction she'd had all night. They'd barely spoken for two minutes, but it was refreshing and light...

And Lauryn fucking Matthews.

Her stomach lurched at the thought. She reached for her laptop and opened it to give herself something else to think about. This had to be her focus. Work. Her family. Her friends. That was enough. The rest just wasn't worth it.

A pair of gentle knocks pulled her attention toward the glass door of her office, and her shared assistant, Arty, pushed his head in. "Happy New Year." Everything from his steely blue eyes to the grin on his pale, adolescent-looking face said he meant it. If he wasn't so damn adorable, Mia might've told him to fuck off.

"Happy New Year, Art."

"Can I get you anything before your eleven o'clock? Coffee?"

"Shit. Coffee." She frowned. "I was supposed to get us all breakfast today."

"I saw you come in this morning, but you were on the phone. Something about not texting 911 unless there's an ambulance on the way. Sounded like a Fantastic Trio thing."

Mia rolled her eyes at the terrible term of endearment he'd given her, Darby and James, and though Darby being stuck outside the house they were currently flipping had hardly been a 911, it had been the best part of Mia's morning. The perfect distraction to rewire her brain before her first meeting. A video conference, thank God, but the second it was over her mind had reverted to Revel's dark entryway and her run-in with Lauryn.

"Anyway," Arty rambled on. "I took care of it. Got you one of those strawberry galette things you like."

"Awesome Arty," Mia muttered the nickname with

sincere affection. "What would we do without you around here?"

"Place would be a madhouse for sure." He stood upright and slid his hands into the pockets of his navy slim fit slacks, looking at her more intently. "You okay, Mia? You seem a little distracted, which is weird, because you kind of always have it together. Like, scary together."

Mia laughed. "There was a compliment in there, right?" She shook her head and waved him off. "I'm fine, Art. Thank you."

Arty nodded. "So, breakfast?"

"Just the coffee, please. French Vanilla, heavy—"

"On the cream. Got it." Art turned on the heels of his cap toe boots, pulling the door shut behind him but stopped. "Oh, she's here, by the way."

Mia creased her forehead, glancing at the time on her laptop. 10:37 a.m. "The client?"

"Ms. Sucre, yes. She seems really nice. Crazy thing though. She's a dead ringer for that—"

"How long has she been out there?" Mia pushed back from her desk and stood. It wasn't often clients showed up early. Twenty minutes early at that. In fact, they'd almost always been late. She was used to being the first person in the room. Last one out. And she'd been in her office for the last hour with nothing to show for it. Arty's casual mention that the client just happened to be there already made her feel unprepared. Tense. Late.

"Five minutes, maybe?" Arty winced. "She asked me not to bother you until eleven. Her word. Bother."

Mia sighed, tapping her blunt, manicured nails against the surface of her desk. "No. I'm sorry." She looked up at Art —his expression wavering between uncertainty and concern. She was wired way too tight this morning, and that was neither Art's fault nor his problem. "Uhm...Give me five and bring her in?"

"Yeah."

"And Art..."

He glanced back at her, his brows raised expectantly.

"Thank you."

"You've got it, Mi."

Mia slid into her chair again and opened the camera on her laptop, checking everything from the arch of her brows to her perfectly lined lips before pulling up the client profile Art had emailed her last week.

Lauren Sucre. *Okay, zero points for that first name*, but Mia had had a conscious bias against literally every variation of it for months already. Besides, this woman had nothing to do with the shit storm that had become her personal life, and the sooner she remembered that the more smoothly this meeting would go.

Seeking a residence, not a rental. Contact number, check. Email, yes.

She fast-tracked to the Needs & Wants section of the doc. Price range, blank. Number of bedrooms, blank. School district... Did this thing not load correctly or was there nothing useful in it?

Her head snapped up at another series of raps on her door. Had it really been five minutes already?

Art entered the room, the woman who Mia assumed to be Ms. Sucre following close behind. Mia's brows drew together as she stood slowly, inadvertently craning her neck for a look at *not* Ms. Sucre.

Lauryn's eyes widened, mouth agape as she stopped in the doorway. Their eyes locked for a moment—Lauryn's amber and fiery beneath the hood of her thick dark brows. Mia reflexively took note of how much better Lauryn looked in the light of her office, her springy dark curls swept up into a messy puff, her skin warm and brown and not buried under layers of winter gear. A low cut top paired with a bomber jacket instead, jeans and boots. When Mia looked up again, Lauryn's expression had lightened. Was she fucking smiling?

Mia straightened her posture. "Whatever this is, I don't have time. Art, please show this person out, and escort Ms. Sucre in *like we agreed*," she gritted out.

"But Mi—"

"Ms. Sucre, Art."

Lauryn placed a hand on Art's shoulder and stepped forward. She was definitely smiling. And Mia was probably, most likely, absolutely about to lose her shit. "Sucre is my legal last name," said Lauryn, extending her hand.

Mia glanced at it like a dirty jockstrap. In her peripheral, she noticed Art discreetly pull the door shut. She wanted to scream at him like she never had, demand he get his skinny metro ass back here, and get this woman out of her sight.

Lauryn retracted her hand. "Are you this polite to all of your clients, or is this the VIP treatment Drew told me about?"

"Drew? As in Dimitrov?" Mia couldn't begin to process this. Drew was a good client. A dream client. She didn't live in Denver, but when she and her husband had been looking for a cabin in Colorado, Mia had gone out of her way to find them the perfect seven-bedroom complete with a fitness room, indoor pool, and wine cellar. It had taken too many flights and a few custom renovations from James and Darby, but when all was done, Drew was happy, and so was the Flippin' Fantastic company account. Besides, the client profile had said Lauren. With an 'e'. "You're the *friend*?"

"Well, I'm more her girlfriend's friend. Blake. But yes,

Drew referred me." Lauryn turned, glancing around Mia's office. "Can't say I'm impressed."

Mia clenched her jaw. Would Darby and James forgive her for punching a prospective client? A celebrity. Would Lauryn sue? She didn't really look like the suing type. Then again, Mia was severely averse to scandal. Hives were breaking out on her back as she stood there.

Lauryn finished her 360 and fixed her eyes on Mia again, her gaze moving down Mia's body then back up. "Aren't you going to say something?"

Mia crossed her arms over her chest. "I could ask you to stop looking at me like you're trying to x-ray my clothes, but you probably can't help yourself."

"Arrogant." Lauryn scoffed. "You look like it, too."

"You know nothing about me."

"I don't." Lauryn shook her head, moving closer. She stopped on the opposite side of Mia's desk, placed both hands on the edge and leaned forward. "I am curious, though." Curly strands of hair dangled against her forehead. Beneath them, her brows knit. "What exactly is it that you *think* you know about me?"

"What do I think I know? Are you fucking kidding me?" Mia glared at her as if she'd sprouted a second head. Was this a joke? Did Lauryn really not know who she was? How do you ruin someone's life and not know who they are? The worst part was, the longer Mia stared at her, the more genuinely confused Lauryn appeared. Maybe there was even the faintest sign of desperation in her eyes—a desire to make sense of the moment. And somehow, Mia felt smaller for it. Small and insignificant and stupid for spending months of her life hating someone who didn't even know she existed; had no idea how they'd hurt her. But it wasn't Lauryn who'd done that, was it?

That was Cori.

Cori was the one who should have known better. Cori was the reason she hadn't gotten out of bed for three days, the reason Darby had to move all her showings for a week and James had to come over and force her to eat.

Cori was the one she'd bought a fucking ring.

But Lauryn...

Lauryn was the person standing in front of her. Lauryn was the client and Mia was resilient—she was—but she wasn't sure she was strong enough for this.

"Excuse me." She rounded her desk and started for the door.

"Sorry, what is happenin—" Lauryn's response got swallowed behind the glass walls.

Mia strutted past Darby's office, ignoring Art's questioning glare as she crossed the lobby toward the bathroom. Their team was small, especially those who came into the office on a daily basis, but she pushed open each stall door anyway. Just to make sure she was alone. Once she'd finally confirmed she was, she brought both hands to the counter and gripped it, grounding herself in the coolness of the surface and its solidity. Her reflection stared back at her—her black hair straightened to perfection, skin bright with reddish-brown undertones and remnants of the spa day she'd had with her mom last week, her makeup flawless. Outside, she looked everything she set out to be. Driven. Professional. Exquisite. Inside, she felt like a ten-car pileup. She closed her eyes and dragged in a breath.

Her phone vibrated against her thigh, the insistence hinting at a phone call. She reached inside her pocket and grabbed it.

Darby.

She swiped her thumb across the screen and brought the phone to her ear. "Hey, Darbs."

"Hold on," Darby greeted. "I have James on the other line."

Mia listened to the silence for a second. Two.

And then James said, "So, what's going on, M?"

"Arty said you didn't look so good when he brought in the client," Darby filled in.

"I believe the word he used was homicidal, actually."

Fucking Arty.

Mia sighed. "Did he tell you the client is Lauryn?"

"Yeah. Sugar or something," mumbled Darby.

"Matthews. Lauryn Matthews is the client. Sucre is her legal name?" Mia explained. She still hadn't made sense of it—how or why any of this was happening.

"Yikes." An image of James cringing flashed in Mia's mind.

"Are you okay?" Darby asked.

Mia turned and leaned against the counter. "Would you guys hate me if I say I couldn't do this?"

"Only a little," James joked.

"You know how I feel about the word hate."

Mia rolled her eyes. "Gee, thanks, guys."

"Of course, we wouldn't hate you, M," Darby replied, "but you're always saying how important big commissions are. This could really help us. Besides, if anyone can handle this, it's you. And we'd be here every step of the way. Just remember you're strong and powerful. You can do hard things!"

"And that neighbor came by asking about permits again."

"Oh my God, did she really?"

"Yup," James deadpanned.

"Ugh." Mia turned to look at herself in the mirror again. She knew if it really came down to it, Darby and James would forgive her for not being able to work with Lauryn. But the more she thought about it, about what they had to deal with on a daily basis—the leaking heater, ripping out an entire wall because the pipes burst—the more she wanted to pull herself together, go back into her office, and start fresh with Lauryn. Darby was right. She *could* do this. She and Lauryn didn't have to like each other. Lauryn needed a house. Mia was in the business of selling houses. It was simple, wasn't it?

"Besides," James said, "what better way to get back at her than to take her money and stick her with an annoying, though alarmingly beautiful neighbor?"

"We should get her a care package," Darby piped in. "A fruit basket."

"Lauryn?"

"No. Zee. The neighbor."

Mia chuckled. "Okay. Why not?" She glanced at the screen of her phone. Nine minutes and counting. She should probably get back if she intended to smooth things over with Lauryn. "I'm going to finish this meeting. Later, babes."

The line went dead.

Mia washed her hands and left the bathroom.

"Uh, Mia?" Art called as she passed his desk.

She held up a finger in his direction. "Give me a minute, Art." When she got to the door of her office, Lauryn was gone.

CHAPTER 4

Lauryn exited the building and reached into her pocket for her phone. Turned out Flippin' Fantastic Real Estate wasn't so fantastic, and she really needed to have a talk with Blake and Drew about the disconnect. The team Drew had described, the trio that had surpassed all expectations to not only find her the perfect cabin but implement all her renovation requests on a ridiculous schedule, Mia Stone could not have been a part of it. If she was, Lauryn wasn't sure she wanted to do business with them. She'd had her share of people forming opinions of her before they'd even met. Mia, though distractingly beautiful, was no exception.

Lauryn paused on the stone pavement, thumbing through her contacts to Blake's number as she slid her free hand into the pocket of her bomber jacket. She glanced up at the scattered clouds across the sky. Hard to believe she was standing in the same city she'd landed in three nights ago. The glacial temperatures and light snow had given way to warmer, more pleasant weather. It was almost as if she'd imagined the whole thing. It certainly hadn't escaped her attention on New Year's Eve that she seemed to be the only

Collide

one who'd been appropriately dressed—all those women at Revel in their cocktail dresses and heels.

Her mind dredged up a memory of Mia. Her straightened hair and precise makeup, even the thigh-length designer coat covering an indubitably short dress. Everything about her screamed unapproachable, except the way she'd smiled at Lauryn in the dimness of that entryway before she'd seen Lauryn's face.

Lauryn pushed the thought out of her mind, hit call on Blake's contact and waited patiently for her to pick up.

"So, are you buying a house up in the Mile High City?" Blake greeted.

"Well, my meeting was a bust so—"

"Lauryn!"

Lauryn grimaced, glancing behind her.

"Really?" The disbelief in Blake's voice barely registered. "What happened?"

Lauryn's eyes stayed with Mia as she closed the gap between them, her gaze shifting from Mia's deep brown irises to the loose fit of her monogram print blouse, skintight hug of her jeans and pair of point-toe pumps on her feet before finding Mia's eyes again. And Lauryn hated every second of it, every instinct to observe her with such attention to detail, because maybe Mia was right—Lauryn couldn't help herself—and Mia didn't deserve the satisfaction.

"Lo?" Blake muttered.

Mia came to a stop in front of Lauryn.

"I'll call you back, B." She blindly disconnected the call and slid her phone into her pocket. "Is this the part where you apologize for whatever just happened back there?"

Mia rolled her eyes. "You're not going to make this easy, are you?"

"Give me one reason I should."

Mia scoffed, licked her lips then bit down on the bottom one. It was almost as if she was genuinely struggling with being there, talking to Lauryn. Lauryn didn't want to take it personally, but this was starting to feel really fucking personal.

"Seriously, what is it you've heard about me? Because we don't know each other, so..." Lauryn trailed off, tilting her head a bit. "Do we know each other?" She didn't have the worst memory, but she had to at least consider it. In the last year alone, with the way her career had taken off, she'd been introduced and reintroduced to hundreds of people. She couldn't possibly remember them all. Yet, somehow, she couldn't help feeling like she would not have forgotten the woman standing in front of her. When Mia still hadn't said anything, Lauryn sighed and shook her head. "Listen, if we've met and I've somehow—"

"We haven't met," said Mia. She stared at Lauryn, her eyes narrowed. Questioning. Searching. Sad?

"Then, what?" The question left Lauryn's lips softer than intended. "You read something about me online? Because I love Taylor as much as the next girl, but I promise despite what she says, not *all* the rumors are true."

Mia's right brow twitched, the movement almost as microscopic as the quirk of her lips. Was that a smile? "I'm sorry. I'm not usually like"—she aimlessly waved one hand in the air—"*that*. I just...Allow me to start over, *please*."

Lauryn bit back a smile at the way the word please definitely hadn't come out easily.

Mia extended her hand. "Mia Stone."

Lauryn ignored the thing in her chest when she accepted the handshake. Kept it terse for both their benefits. "Lauryn."

"Um." Mia pushed a few strands of her hair behind one ear and glanced back at the building. She cleared her throat then looked at Lauryn again. "Should we go back inside? Continue this in my office."

"I'm good here, if you don't mind. That bench over there seems fine."

Mia's jaw tensed as she eyed the wooden bench off to their right. Lauryn didn't need to know her well to know she despised the suggestion, that she would much rather ride the elevator four floors back to her office and settle in behind her glass walls and immaculate space with its color-coded minimalist shelves and not-a-pen-out-of-place desk. Up there, she was in control, and Lauryn got the impression that was exactly the way she liked it. Down here, out in the open, she looked a little off her game, maybe even the slightest bit vulnerable. Lauryn preferred it that way. At least for now.

"Right." Mia's face twisted into a Halloween mask of a smile. "Okay, then."

Lauryn tried to contain her amusement as they got seated, Mia faced forward, Lauryn angled with an arm on the back of the bench so she could look at Mia directly.

"So," Mia started, "I noticed you left a lot of the paperwork blank, questions I need answers to if we're to get you exactly what you want."

"What questions?"

"Well, do you know how many bedrooms you'd like?"

Lauryn shrugged. "I live alone. Doesn't matter."

"Okay. What about neighborhoods? Would you like something in the city or the suburbs?"

"The suburbs are fine." Lauryn took a casual glance around. "I guess the city doesn't seem too bad either."

Mia's jaw clenched. "What's your price range?"

"Flexible."

"*Lauryn*," Mia huffed, crossing her legs as she turned so they were face-to-face. "What is happening here?"

"What...do you mean?" Lauryn asked cautiously. An echo of the way Mia said her name replayed in her mind. Even said like that, with obvious frustration, she kind of liked it. And okay, really, what *was* happening here?

"I mean, are you really here to buy a house? Because you don't seem to have given this much thought, and it's kind of a big deal."

Of course, it was a big deal. Lauryn knew that. But maybe she hadn't given it *so* much thought. Maybe it had been Christmas eve and Blake and Drew were being disgustingly adorable, talking about brunch with one family and dinner with the other, and Lauryn had felt inescapably nostalgic. She didn't have much family. She had Sully, and Sully was here. So when she mentioned maybe buying a house in Denver someday and Drew said, "Oh my God, I know an *amazing* real estate company there," she'd decided that someday was next week. This was someday.

She glanced skyward, swallowing. "Is it something we can figure out together? Is that not how this works?"

"Less often than not," Mia answered. She closed her eyes and rubbed at her temples, then sighed almost as if she'd resigned herself to the idea that this was not going to be easy. "But yes," she said, looking at Lauryn again. "I'm sure we can figure it out."

Lauryn held her gaze, searching, and for a second, the slightest bit longer, Mia's countenance softened, and her lips parted. Lauryn became acutely aware of her own breathing, the slow thud of her heartbeat. She wasn't sure what she was getting from Mia, from herself even, but this wasn't the person Drew had described—the charming, confident realtor who had found Drew's dream cabin. "We can do this another time," Lauryn offered.

Mia blinked. "Why?" She shook her head. "I mean, yes, if you have somewhere to be."

"I don't. It's just..." Lauryn narrowed her gaze. "Don't take this the wrong way, but I'm kind of getting two vibes from you here, and neither seem fit for selling houses."

"Oh, so you're a psychic, too?" Mia scoffed, standing.

"Mia." Lauryn grabbed her hand and they both glanced down at the gesture. "Sorry," Lauryn murmured, letting go. She really needed to stop doing that. "I'm sorry," she said louder. "What I meant was, this doesn't seem to be going well. You're probably having a bad...*whatever*, and I'm not due back in LA for a few weeks. I'd be happy to reschedule if you have some time. If not," Lauryn smiled, "I can honestly say I've had better first impressions, but also, I've probably made worse, so it was nice to meet you, anyway."

Mia frowned, the look in her eyes unreadable. Not the anger or sadness that had been fluctuating over the course of their entire interaction. Lauryn couldn't decide if that was better or worse. She didn't know why she'd said anything she just had, except maybe that Mia didn't seem okay. And Lauryn couldn't sit in that. She didn't want Mia to have to either.

"Tomorrow," Mia said softly.

"Tomorrow?"

She nodded. "Can you be here tomorrow?"

"Yes, of course."

At that, Mia smiled, and Lauryn wasn't sure what she'd said but she wanted to say it again. "You're not going to ask me what time?"

Lauryn stood, bringing herself eye-level with Mia again. "What time?"

"I think I have an opening at midday, but let me confirm and have my assistant give you a call?"

Something about those words bothered Lauryn. She wasn't sure if it was because Mia was the kind of boss who had her assistant make all her calls, or because despite every instance of Mia being less than kind since the moment she had recognized Lauryn at Revel, Lauryn still hoped Mia would be the one to call. What did it say about her that the first woman she felt any desire to get to know in months was someone who had barely managed to be kind to her? Another thing to hash out with her therapist.

"Lauryn?"

"Yeah." She fabricated a smile. "That sounds good."

"Okay." Mia turned to leave, the heels of her red bottoms just audible on the pavement. It wasn't until she'd made it to the door that she glanced at Lauryn again.

Lauryn planted her feet more firmly, though she could feel something inside her shift, her anticipation building.

Mia looked away and faded beyond the glass doors.

CHAPTER 5

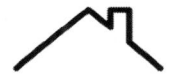

As far as first days back at the office went, this had easily been one of Mia's worst. She'd managed to make it through her only showing—a quaint four-bedroom in Hale—and actually close the sale. She was off, though, and she knew it. She'd all but skated through on mechanical charm and the relationship she'd already cultivated with the Davidsons. Now that it was over and she was back in her office, she couldn't help the constant loop of thoughts unraveling in her mind. She'd left her call with James and Darby with every intention of keeping it together. But every time she so much as looked at Lauryn, her focus would falter, and the undercurrent of rage and pain she'd been trying to suppress would burn its way to the surface. Couldn't she have pretended for an hour?

No matter who Lauryn was, deals like this were important for their company, especially only three years into getting it off the ground. Sure, they'd been lucky enough to build a steady clientele through the local market, but celebrity contracts didn't only mean the possibility of seven-figure commissions. They also came with the promise of another. For better or worse, people like Lauryn Matthews were well-connected, and they talked. Isn't that how Lauryn had come to be in her office in the first place? Because she knew Drew. Correction: Knew Drew's girlfriend.

Mia literally couldn't afford to fuck this up. If it was anyone else, she would have already lost her chance. If it was anyone else, she wouldn't be this much of a mess in the first place. She reclined in her chair and closed her eyes. The image flashed in her mind.

A dimly lit dungeon of a lounge. The spread of marijuana, pills and cocaine on the corner table amidst a myriad of blurred faces. Lauryn. The woman on her lap with her curly dyed-blonde hair swept up into a messy bun, back turned to the camera leaving the honey bee tattoo at the nape of her neck on full display. Same tattoo Cori had. Same weekend Cori had been in LA for an art show with friends.

Mia sat upright and closed her laptop on the window of unread emails she'd yet to make her way through. She couldn't do this again. Not after weeks of barely keeping it together and finally getting Cori to stop texting, calling, showing up at the apartment. Not after Mia had left that apartment to start fresh. She slipped her computer into her winged leather tote and exited her office.

Arty perked up as she came to a stop by his desk. His gaze drifted to the bag in her hand before meeting hers again.

"I'll be out the rest of the day. Please hold my calls," Mia instructed.

Art nodded. "Sure thing, boss."

Mia winced, starting toward the elevator. "You know I hate it when you call me that." She pushed the button and waited.

"Anything else you need? You don't have any other meetings today, but do you need things moved around for tomorrow? Wednesday maybe?"

"No. Oh." She stepped into the elevator and turned to face him again. "Ms. Sucre"—she tried not to visibly cringe at the way that tasted in her mouth, or think about why the alternative was better—"*Lauryn* is now my 12 o'clock tomorrow."

"Okay." Another ardent nod. "I'll put that in. Should I call and confirm?"

"No. I'll take care of it." After the way they'd left things earlier, maybe Lauryn would take Mia calling as an act of good faith. "And Art..." She stopped the closing elevator doors with one hand. "I know you're only trying to help, but if you report this to Darby and James, you are so fired."

"Got it, Mi."

MIA PULLED into the brick driveway and parked. She'd always loved this neighborhood—the tree-lined streets and verdant lawns—and Matthieu and Layla's recently renovated home was the picture of transitional architecture. Classic meets modern aesthetics. It had Darby and James all over it.

Mia reached into her bag and grabbed her phone to send Matt a text.

I'm coming over.

Her phone buzzed with a reply almost instantly.

Funny. Could've sworn it was your red bimmer just pulling in.

Mia rolled her eyes, fingers swift across her keyboard. *Garnet.*

Still obnoxious.

Still haven't asked your opinion.
Mhm. So, are you coming in or what?

She chuckled to herself, reaching for her bag as she pushed the door open. The sun had reached its afternoon high, the sky clearer now, but the air had retained a pleasant chill that felt distinct to this time of year. Her favorite time of year. It occurred to her that besides the three days she'd spent with her family for Christmas, she hadn't really taken any time to enjoy it. Even her schedule was designed to dwell in the holidays—the first two days back always exceptionally light, giving her time to recalibrate. There were few things she hated more than an inbox full of unread emails. Yet here she was randomly showing up on her brother's doorstep at three in the afternoon and ignoring 246 of them. Maybe she should talk to James and Darby about taking the week off between Christmas and New Year like Matt's firm did. They'd totally go for it. Okay, Darby would go for it. James on the other hand...

Matt slid open one panel of the stacking doors leading to the family room and stood in the doorway, grinning. His sleek low cut hair and beard looked recently groomed, and his plain beige T-shirt hugged his biceps with all the vanity he liked to scold in Mia, but even at well over six feet, his too-long-jeans dragged beneath his bare feet. If only his corporate law clients could see him now. "Missed me?"

"Missed my niece and nephew," Mia corrected. "You're just the goofy gatekeeper."

Like clockwork, Isabella darted round the bend to the dining room, screaming "Aunt Mia," and wrapped her arms around Mia's legs. A bit slower to the party, Isaac appeared, gracefully crash-landing against the wooden floors and picking himself up in a second.

"Hi, babies."

Bella peered up at her through a mess of dark curls, eyes dreamy and brown. "Zac's a baby, but not me." Right. Six years old was the pinnacle of adulthood these days.

Isaac clapped his little hands and babbled, "*Bay-bie!*"

Mia smiled, stooping down to their level—not an easy feat in five-inch pumps. "So, how's my big kid doing?" she asked Bella. "Ready for school next week?"

"Yes! I've already packed my bag and picked my colors for the days."

Isaac ambled over and started tugging at the straps of Mia's bag. Givenchy. But how much damage could a toddler do?

Mia tilted her head at Bella. "What do you mean, sweetie?"

"She color-coded her closet for each day of the week," Matt explained. "This is the kind of influence you have on my child."

Mia's brows raised as she stood, still looking up at her brother even with the five-inch advantage. She lowered her voice when she asked, "You let a six-year-old organize her own closet?"

"Like mom and dad could stop you."

"Fair point."

Bella wrapped a hand around hers. "Do you want to see?"

"In a second, love. Layla around?"

Matt shut the door and Mia just registered how much cozier it was inside, especially with the fireplace lit. "Kick boxing class."

"Ah." Mia smirked. "For when you act up?"

"Hilarious."

"I'd totally take her side."

"So loyal."

"It's the least I could do. She did make my two favorite humans."

"Hu-man," Isaac tested.

Matthieu scoffed. "Uh huh. Just her?"

"I mean, you helped, but don't hold out for a trophy, Matt."

"Aunt Mia," Bella singsonged, tugging at Mia's hand.

Mia laughed, shoving Matt on the shoulder. "Okay, Bells. Think I've roasted your dad enough for one day." She took a few steps toward the sofa and rested her bag there.

Bella led her toward the stairs. "What's roasted?"

"Oh, don't worry, sweetie. Tell me about your colors." She brushed her free hand through Bella's hair, more than happy to devote all her attention to Bella's latest fascination. Thoughts of Lauryn lingered in her mind. Lauryn and Cori, and work. She couldn't avoid it forever. She didn't intend to. All she needed was a few hours to forget, and Bella and Isaac had always been first-rate distractions. Tonight, she'd brainstorm. She'd make a plan to find Lauryn the perfect residence in two weeks—less, even—and put it all behind her for good.

It was well after seven by the time Mia had decided she'd let herself off the hook enough for one day. She'd completed a thorough tour of Bella's clothing choices for the next week, which happened to include all three primary colors and only variations of purple thereafter, and okay... maybe Matt was right to be a little concerned. Of all the things Mia wished to pass on to her niece, her proclivity for organizing with habits that could easily pass as compulsive was not one of them. Neither was the perfectionism, materialism nor any of her other *isms* for that matter. Isaac, at least, was happy enough to fumble around with the shapes of his wooden block set until they fit, minus the pentagon still lying on the floor of his nursery, riddled with teeth marks.

Matt loaded the final dish into the washer and grabbed a towel to dry his hands as he faced Mia. "So, you ready to tell me what's going on?"

Mia fixed her eyes on her laptop and slid it further to the edge of the island counter, opening another email. "What do you mean?" She'd been expecting him to ask since the moment Layla had taken the kids upstairs for bed, and yet, feigning ignorance was instinct. So much for the path of least resistance.

"You only show up like this when you need them to tire you out, and I mean, thanks—there's only so many times I can read *Hair Love* before I start reciting it in my sleep—but what kind of big brother would I be if I didn't ask."

Mia squinted at him in amusement. "I'll make sure Layla gets that on recording."

"Quit dodging."

"I'm not."

Matt pulled a face.

"Okay, fine." Mia sighed, shaking her head. "I have a tough client. Like, for the first time, I think I'm scared I won't be able to do *my job*."

"What do you mean?" Matt leaned against the counter and folded his arms.

"She's..." Mia trailed off, trying to think of the right words to explain. She'd never exactly told her family why she'd broken off the engagement with Cori, settling instead for the explanation of how they'd rushed into it and had realized they weren't as compatible as they thought. They'd swallowed it easily enough. She'd only told them exactly what they already thought.

"Wait," Matt closed the space to the opposite end of the

island in two steps and leaned his elbows against it, grinning conspiratorially. "Is this it? The reason you break that ridiculous no dating clients rule?"

"What?" Mia scrunched up her face. "Ew. And that's not a ridiculous rule."

"It is in real estate. She's hot, isn't she?" His grin widened. "Oh, you should see the panic on your face."

"Matthieu, stop it. She's not…I'm mean, she's not *not*—Ugh." Mia clenched her jaw. "I'm not doing this with you." She closed her laptop—would she ever make it through these fucking emails today?—and stood, slipping it into her bag. As if she was going to be goaded by her brother into even considering Lauryn as attractive after everything that's happened. So what if she had perfect bone structure and gorgeous skin, and fiery amber eyes that kind of—

"Come on." Matt laughed. "You can't go without telling me why this woman has clearly gotten under your skin, especially if she could be my future sister-in-law."

"You're a child."

"Can you blame me? It's not like you've dated anyone since—"

"I went speed dating on Saturday."

"You did *what*?"

Mia faced him as she got to the door. "Darbs took me and James."

"That…actually explains everything."

"Mhm. It was hell and I only filled one of my cards so it wouldn't feel like a complete waste of time, so don't go planning any double dates yet." She pushed the door open and stepped into the chill night air, immediately clutching her arms closer to her body. "Anyway, I have some work to catch up on before bed."

Matt followed, walking her out to her car. "Call mom. See if you can get her to stay off her damn feet more."

"You know she doesn't listen to me either, right?" Mia slid into the driver's seat and started the engine.

"She doesn't listen to anyone, Mia. We tell her anyway."

"Yes, we do." She glanced up at him, offering a sincere, "Thanks for dinner."

"Anytime, sis." Matt tapped his hand against the open window of Mia's car before stepping back. "And Mi, about this client...Remember what dad always says?"

Mia smiled, instantly understanding. "Business is—"

"Never personal," Matt finished.

Mia laughed, shifting her car into *drive*. "Yeah." As she pulled out of the driveway, she couldn't help feeling like this was the one time it *was* personal.

CHAPTER 6

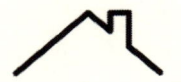

Lauryn absentmindedly strummed her guitar as the TV played muted in the background. Some Hallmark movie she'd lost interest in within the first ten minutes. It'd been at least a month since she'd picked up her guitar or sat in front of the piano. Today, inspiration niggled at her like a stubborn headache. She didn't have words for whatever wanted to get out—not yet anyway—but its gentle insistence made it impossible to shake. At least earlier when her manager had called for his exasperating albeit typical check-in of "How's the writing going?" and she'd droned, "Fine, Ken," this time it wasn't entirely a lie.

She wasn't touring right now, but maybe she'd never really given herself a proper break from the constant stage that was LA. She loved spending time with Blake and Drew, but she didn't know how Drew did it all the time with the cameras everywhere, especially after the Luxe article had dropped. After the Instagram thing, it was like they'd followed Lauryn around just to catch her screwing up again.

New Artist of the Year nominee Lauryn Matthews throws drug-fueled after party!

"Sources say the singer songwriter has had an issue with substance abuse for years..."

Lauryn's grip tightened on her guitar and she abruptly stopped strumming. *Sources.* She scoffed. She'd smoked what? One joint her entire life. When she was *nineteen*. But that's not what the headlines said, what the articles suggested, and the media never got it wrong. Sometimes she wondered if that was all people saw when they looked at her now.

Was that what Mia saw? Why every look she gave Lauryn seemed fueled with rage, disappointment and sadness.

"Giving a lot of credit to someone who's barely even met you, Lo," she grumbled to herself. Not to mention how well she'd inserted herself into Mia's thoughts. Textbook narcissist.

She slid forward on the L of the sofa and put the guitar next to her. So much for inspiration. She grabbed the remote and started flicking through the channels.

A buzzing stirred against the coffee table, and she reached for her phone instead, furrowing her brows at the local area code. The only person she knew in Denver was Sully and Sully's number had been saved in her phone since she'd gotten her first one at fifteen years old. Mia's assistant was supposed to call to confirm their meeting tomorrow, but almost nine o'clock at night didn't seem right. She hit the green button and brought the phone to her ear anyway. "This is Lauryn."

"Lauryn, hi."

Lauryn's stomach dropped and she creased her forehead, stating more than asking when she said, "Mia."

"Yeah. It's late. I'm sorry. It's just...Our meeting."

"Tomorrow. Midday, right?"

"Yes. I never had Art confirm like I promised."

"That's okay." Lauryn wanted to say she was glad Mia had called instead, however late, but she wasn't sure how Mia would take it. She didn't want to mistake the calm in Mia's tone for something more positive. If anything, she was probably exhausted. Mia's sigh all but confirmed it, and Lauryn readied herself for a 'good night'.

"Listen, Lauryn, I wanted to apologize again for what happened this morning. I was completely unprofessional, and I don't expect you to forgive it, but I can promise to help you find and build someplace that will feel like home before you even set foot in it. Whatever that looks or feels like, we'll make it happen. My partners Darby and James love a good challenge."

A faint smile tugged at Lauryn's lips. This was the pitch she'd been expecting. Before she could stop herself, or consider why she would even want to, she said, "Somewhere that feels like the place family comes home to."

Mia stayed silent.

"You know, like, for Thanksgiving and Christmases. That's what I want."

"Okay?" Mia mumbled uncertainly.

"I know that still doesn't help but—"

"No. It does." Mia paused. "That's great, Lauryn. Keep thinking about it. I'm going to call it a night and be sure to make this my only call to you outside office hours."

Lauryn didn't mind. Not even a little. She didn't say that either, but she couldn't help asking, "Did it get better?"

"I'm sorry?"

"Your day."

"Oh. Um—yes, actually. It did."

"I'm glad," Lauryn answered softly.

"Good night, Lauryn."

"Night, Mia." When the line went dead, Lauryn put her phone down, reached for her guitar and picked up her strumming again.

Lauryn shut the door of her rental SUV and started toward Flippin' Fantastic. The "Box of Sunshine Gift Box" in her hands served as a palpable reminder of the strange impulse that had overcome her ten minutes ago when she'd given herself the work of finding parking in Downtown Denver at almost midday to go find it. Admittedly, she was unsure what she'd been looking for when she'd climbed out of her car and immersed herself among the vibrant offering of boutiques and gift shops within her current radius. It all seemed so... walkable, and since she hadn't yet developed the diva quality to offset her need to be early to absolutely everything, she'd had time to burn.

There was something dangerous about the way Mia slid into her thoughts at the most unexpected moments. Something involuntary and powerful in its unsophistication that made her feel like a teenager with a crush on the cheerleader who would never notice her. She was self-aware enough to identify it, especially since she'd stayed up well into the morning writing lyrics about strangers who collide then spend a night walking the city like they'd known each other forever. A crush. Laughable, really. She'd sworn off them a year into watching Blake pine over Drew back in college. All those nights they'd gotten a little too drunk trying to forget. Besides, her love life had gotten a lot less complicated once she realized lots of beautiful women wanted to bed a broody musician. Then again, Blake wound up with the woman of her dreams and Lauryn was... alone, in Denver, randomly buying sunshine gift boxes for her fucking realtor.

She stopped at the entrance, half-considering turning around and dumping it into the nearest trash can.

The door swung open and a woman nodded a greeting, stepping by Lauryn and holding the door open.

Lauryn forced a tight-lipped smile and hurried inside. Instinctively, she did a quick take of the lobby before deciding that this didn't have to be weird. It could just be a peace offering. An accompaniment to their do-over. Maybe the start of a friendship? So, Mia was beautiful. She also happened to be quick-tempered and kind of an asshole, and if Lauryn wasn't completely and irrationally beguiled based on those two minutes in Revel the other night, she would be asking Sully for recommendations for another realtor right now. She pushed the button to the elevator, and the doors slid open with an audible hum. The four-floor ascent went by in a blink, a ding and then she was met with the boyish grin of Mia's assistant.

"Ms. Sucre." He stood from behind his desk and started toward her.

Lauryn smiled, though hearing people call her by her last name always hit with a dose of ambivalence. "Lauryn, please."

"Right. Lauryn. May I take your..." He trailed off, his expression shifting as he glanced down. "Box of sunshine?"

Lauryn's chuckle was reflexive. "I'm fine. Thanks." She slipped her phone out of her pocket to check the time—three minutes to spare—then signaled toward the empty waiting area. "I'm just going to sit, if that's okay."

"Well, uh, actually Mia asked me to bring you in as soon as you were here."

"Oh." Unexpected. Lauryn bobbed her head in assent. "Okay."

"Awesome. This way, please."

Lauryn walked with Arty down the short hallway, past only one other office—empty just as it had been yesterday. The name on the door stood out this time though—Jane Darby—and she recalled with taunting clarity Mia identifying this partner only by their last name when they'd spoken last night. She wondered if that was the version of Mia she was walking toward, if she'd be met with the same soothing calmness that made her want to keep Mia on the phone all night.

Art slowed, raising a hand to knock on Mia's door and Lauryn purposely stayed a step behind him.

"Yes, Arty?"

"Lauryn's here." He stepped aside and Lauryn moved into the doorway.

Mia stood slowly. "Lauryn..." Her gaze dropped to the screen of her laptop. "Right on time." Like yesterday, her raven hair framed her face with a single middle part, her makeup precise from the arch of her brows and liner around her eyes to her full lips. Red today. Teasingly red.

"This is, um—" Lauryn closed the distance to Mia's desk and offered the box. "This is for you."

"Oh?" Mia cleared her throat, examining the contents of the box as she accepted it.

"The cookies are homemade. And the candle is hand poured, whatever that means. The tea and honey sticks are supposedly really good, and the succulent—" Lauryn glanced around Mia's office. No plants. "Well, I guess you could put that in the lobby or something."

"Lauryn—"

"I know you said your day already got better yesterday. I just saw it and I don't know. Box of sunshine...seemed nice, I guess."

Ugh. This was weird. She was totally making it weird.

Mia plucked out the card and raised a perfectly arched brow at it. "A little box of sunshine to brighten your day as you always brighten mine. *Probably. In the future. When you find me a house.*"

"The last part wasn't included," Lauryn clarified. Although, the fact that it had been scribbled in not-so-clean-handwriting at the bottom of the card was probably a giveaway.

Mia stared at her for a moment, and it was almost as if she was thinking *what the fuck?* But a smile tugged at her lips, ever so slightly, and she burst into a full-on laugh.

And okay, Lauryn was completely gone. Put her on the Blake program. Five years of pining for a lifetime of *this*.

"Lauryn, wha..." Mia breathed, still chuckling. "You got me a succulent?"

Lauryn licked her lips, powerless to do anything but stare and smile, too. "As much as you clearly wanted to rip my head off yesterday, you also seemed kind of...sad? I don't know. I've heard I'm an empath, if you can believe it."

Mia's smile faded, a row of well cared for teeth disappearing behind her lips.

Fuck. What had that taken, two seconds, Lo? "Or just think of it as a peace offering."

"No." Mia shook her head as if to rid herself of some unwelcomed thought or confusion. "It's lovely, really. Thank you, Lauryn."

"Don't mention it."

The moment dragged, Lauryn trapped in the deep

brown of Mia's eyes, and Mia seemingly in search of something Lauryn was happy to let her uncover. She didn't have secrets. No point. Too many vultures to sniff them out and sell them to the highest bidder. She had angst, yes. Anxiety, tenfold. Reservations. These days, who didn't?

Mia visibly swallowed and pulled her gaze away, staring at the gift box even after she'd set it down. "I wanted to take you somewhere. For a showing, I mean." She looked up at Lauryn with recovered cavalier. "We could sit here and go through all those questions again, but there's little point in it if you don't know what you want."

Lauryn knew what she wanted, but they were talking about houses, right? She offered a hopefully casual shrug. "Sure."

"I'll show you three of our units, different styles and neighborhoods, and we'll talk about what you like in each. That way, we can narrow things down a bit." Mia picked up the gift box, apparently having decided it would be better suited in an open space on a shelf across the room.

Lauryn followed the slow tap of her heels up her form-fitting ankle pants and elegant long-sleeved blouse that had replaced yesterday's marginally more casual getup.

"When were you hoping to move in?"

"Uh...As soon as possible, I guess. I do have to be back in LA in a couple of weeks, but I'll be back and forth either way." She'd only booked her townhouse for a month, but she could always extend or find somewhere else. Stay with Sully if it came to it.

"Okay. One of the units I had in mind was recently acquired, so we only just started renovation. Considering you're in a bit of a rush, we'll see that one last."

"No rush."

Mia squinted. "Are you always this incongruous?"

Lauryn matched her stare. "Have you always been the kind of person to use words like incongruous in casual conversation?"

"This isn't casual." Mia turned to her desk, picked up her cell phone then reached into her bag and came up with a key fob on her index finger, leaving her manicured nails on display. "Should we go?"

Lauryn wasn't sure she'd ever heard a question in a more demanding tone or met anyone so beautifully intense and layered. She had no idea if Mia would ever see her as more than a client, but somehow, she knew she'd find out.

CHAPTER 7

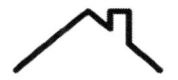

THE DRIVE OVER TO THE TOWNHOUSE HAD BEEN QUIETER THAN Mia expected. Being stuck with Lauryn for God knows how long would be difficult enough as it was. In her presence, Cori was everywhere—her delicate Korean features and London accent vivid in Mia's imagination, her vibrancy and untamed youth, the way she was the kind of passionate that drew in everything and everyone, like a wildfire. God, how had Mia ever thought proposing was a good idea?

She tightened her grip on the steering wheel of her car and glanced over at Lauryn. Lauryn who threw drug-fueled Hollywood parties and fucked other people's fiancés without regard. Lauryn who had cared enough to ask about Mia's day and had shown up to their meeting holding a box of fucking sunshine. Mia couldn't reconcile the two, and she didn't like it one bit. She needed to hate her to get through this. Get through it again. For as long as she'd known herself, she'd strived on certainty and getting distracted with questions about who the real Lauryn Matthews was wouldn't help her move on, and it sure wouldn't help her do her job. Yet, she was beginning to realize that the two were irreversibly intertwined, especially since Lauryn barely had any idea what she wanted in a property. What kind of person just picks up and decides to buy a house without even considering what they want?

"You okay, Mia?"

"What?" It probably echoed a bit harsher than intended.

Lauryn replied unphased. "You kind of have a death grip on the wheel there."

Mia scoffed, but loosened her grip. "You pay a lot of attention to me for someone I've just met."

"You're kind of difficult to not pay attention to."

"What does that even mean?" Mia glanced at her, Lauryn's eyes fixed her way now, then a thought hit. "Was that a line? Famous singer casually flirts, women swoon."

Lauryn laughed—full and hearty—and Mia's chest tightened in a way she wanted to rip out of her memory right that second. "I'm hardly famous, and you don't really seem like the swooning type. Besides, if I was flirting with you, you wouldn't have to wonder."

Mia pursed her lips, suddenly annoyed she'd kept her blazer on for the drive. She reached across the dash and turned down the heat as she slowed at a stoplight. "Whatever, Lauryn. As long as the lines are clear here. I'm your realtor, not your groupie, and *nothing* you say will make me just fall into your lap."

"Hmm. So you have been following the rumors."

Mia spun in her seat. The staunch professional in her screamed for her to pause, reel it in, *business is never personal*, but she couldn't let that one go, especially when she knew exactly who the woman pictured in Lauryn's lap was. "Are you denying it?"

"Why do you care?"

The meadows of fire flickering in her eyes made Mia want to recoil from the burn. Now, six months ago. It was too late either way. "I don't."

"Real convincing. You want to get to know someone, Mia, the internet's not the way. And if you have something to ask me? I'm right here."

The moment stretched between them—Lauryn's glare unwaveringly intense—and Mia almost wanted to come out with the whole thing. Why was she keeping it a fucking secret anyway? She hadn't done anything wrong. But that was it, wasn't it? There were two people in that picture, but only one of them had made Mia a promise. That person wasn't sitting in her car right now. Maybe that's what bothered her, that a part of her knew her anger was misdirected. Because maybe Lauryn *didn't* know, and if Mia didn't hate her, there was a very real possibility that Lauryn might be likable?

Lauryn leaned back in her chair, facing the road again. "The light's green."

MIA DIDN'T LIKE BEING STUCK in a car with offhandedly silent Lauryn, but silently seething Lauryn was giving her an aneurysm. By the time she'd finally pulled up in front of the two-bedroom townhouse, she was so wired, she'd slammed her car door shut with a force that would make her want to strangle anyone else. Lauryn spared a fleeting look Mia's way, her brows knit, lips straight as she stepped onto the curb and slipped both hands into the pockets of her fashionably oversized bomber. Was she seriously not going to say anything? Hang on to this guilt trip plan of convincing Mia she had somehow misjudged her?

Well, fuck that. Mia felt no guilt. None. Zero. And Lauryn could go fuck herself.

"Isn't this the part where you're supposed to say something about the house?" Lauryn mumbled.

Mia forcefully restrained an eye-roll, digging deep for a tone that would pass as calm. "So we're pretty much in the heart of Denver, just a few minutes from the Denver Art Museum, and more dining than you will probably ever need. But one of the amazing things about this unit—apart from the recent renovation—is the private rooftop patio. Incredible view."

Lauryn bobbed her head. "Cool."

Mia narrowed her gaze, actually rolling her eyes when she started toward the entrance. "Let's go inside." She pushed the door open, Lauryn following into the modest foyer, and she immediately delved into her spiel on the first floor. They swept through the two-car garage, office and foremost bathroom quickly before moving to the open plan second floor, where signs of the renovations were most obvious. The Ashwood flooring gleamed with a recent polish, complemented by a top of the line two-door refrigerator, range oven and dishwasher.

Lauryn stood by the windows in the breakfast nook, hands still in her pocket as she peered down at something outside. Perfectly underwhelmed by it all. Not that Mia would know exactly, given that Lauryn had only reluctantly mumbled an acknowledgement every few sentences and refused to even look at Mia directly since the moment they'd set foot inside.

Mia had had showings with clients that were distracted or maybe just looking for something else, but Lauryn had given her literally nothing to work with, and the least she could do was act like she was paying attention.

"How many bedrooms did you say there were?"

Mia almost missed the question. "Two," she answered, reflexively taking a few steps toward Lauryn. "Third floor. You mentioned you lived alone, and you are someone of certain renown, so a private rooftop lounge and four bathrooms would be great for hosting."

"Right."

"As for what you said last night..." Mia cleared her throat, sorting through the fog of the memory. It wasn't only the phrasing of her question that reverberated with uncomfortable intimacy, it was the call, too—the way Lauryn's voice went up when she realized it had been Mia calling, the patience in her tone and vulnerability in her confession of what she wanted in a house. A home. Something Mia, admittedly, was not only caught off guard by, but understood all too well. "How big of a family are we talking?"

Lauryn shrugged, still looking out the window. "Not big."

"Well, do you have any siblings?"

"No." She turned and crossed back to the island in the kitchen.

"Um..." Mia glanced around the room, almost as if to give herself time to understand. Lauryn had said *somewhere that feels like the place family comes home to,* right? "So, just your parents then?"

"No parents."

"I—I don't understand. I thought you sai—"

Lauryn scoffed, sinking her teeth into her bottom lip. "What? Your Google brief didn't cover me being raised in foster care?"

Mia's expression went slack, and something dreadful settled in the pit of her stomach. That wouldn't have been in the client profile, and despite what Lauryn clearly thought,

Mia hadn't done a deep dive into her background. In fact, after those three days following the Instagram thing, she hadn't looked into Lauryn at all—Darby had made sure her search results didn't populate a single site with Lauryn's name, right after Mia had unfollowed all of Cori's social media and deleted her number. Really, all she'd done was rewatch the fifteen-second clip an unhealthy number of times, reminding herself why both Cori and by extension, Lauryn Matthews, were dead to her. It's not like it hurt more, rewatching it. It's not like it *could* hurt more. But this... The look of accusation on Lauryn's face, the dullness in her ever-glowing eyes, Mia didn't know what to do with any of it. If she understood what Lauryn had said though, and it all seemed pretty cut and dry, she wouldn't wish that void, that sense of longing Lauryn clearly felt on anyone. She stepped forward. "Lauryn, I—"

"It doesn't even matter." Lauryn shook her head. "This isn't it."

"What isn't it?"

"The house, Mia. It's great, really. It just—" She sighed. "This isn't it."

"Okay," Mia said softly. "There are other options, of course. We can set up another showing, or I can try to carve out a couple of hours next week and we can see a few."

"Yeah. Let me know what time. I'll make it work."

"Lauryn—"

Lauryn winced. "Don't say whatever you're about to say. I can already hear it in your voice. Guess you really didn't know. I'm sorry for going off like that. Weird topic."

"Yeah. Of course."

Lauryn tapped her hand on the counter and glanced out the windows again. "If we're done here, I think I'm just going to head out."

Mia nodded. "Sure. I'll drive you back."

"I actually think I'm going to grab a Lyft or something."

"Yeah. Yeah, okay."

Lauryn started toward the stairs, and Mia stood by helplessly, watching her go. If only she had longer than a few seconds to settle her thoughts, make sense of exactly what she was feeling, maybe she could have found words to recover the moment. Then again, what moment would that be—the wasted ones they'd spent fighting on their way over, outside when she stood by waiting for Lauryn to say something instead, or this one? The moment she'd realized maybe she'd put too much stock in whatever she thought she knew about Lauryn Matthews. Based on what? A fifteen-second video and the dozen articles that had memorialized a night of bad decisions? The thing was, those fifteen seconds had ripped a lifetime from Mia, and she clearly wasn't over that. But maybe Lauryn was right. Mia didn't *know* her, and she didn't want to. So why did it bother her so much that Lauryn had left without even saying goodbye?

CHAPTER 8

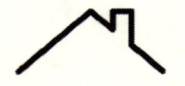

Lauryn tucked her arms closer to her body, shifting her hands around in the pocket of her jacket as she and Sully walked toward Sushi Den. The air had a bite to it—not freezing exactly—but she was beginning to think chilly was typical of winter nights in Denver. She hadn't needed her quilted, walker jacket since New Year's Eve, so it was probably safe to say she was adjusting. Although, tonight happened to be the first night since then she'd even bothered to go out. The last three had drug on with the same stream of thoughts. The showing of the townhouse on Tuesday. Her argument with Mia. Arguments. Her parents—where they were, who they were, why they weren't here. All punctuated by lyric-less humming and strumming. Then lyrics the label would never approve, and Ken's voice in her head. "None of that mopey-dopey shit, Lo. People are sad, the world is broken. They don't want reminders. They want distraction. Give 'em more of *Rush*." Because God forbid she evolve beyond the "bangers" the label had decided would suit her *image*. Sometimes, she wondered if he remembered how he'd discovered her—in a drab LA lounge, singing a

Cary Brothers cover to a roaring crowd of seven, and the bartender.

Sully's shoulder brushed hers as they rounded a bend from the parking lot to a quaint single-story brick building. "Best sushi in Denver." She grinned. "The country even."

Lauryn cracked a smile at the glint in Sully's eyes, her green irises almost indistinguishable beneath the night sky. "How do you look like a little kid on Christmas right now?"

Sully shrugged. "You're as young as you feel."

"Right. 'Cause that's how that works."

Lauryn peered up at a wispy, leafless tree wrapped in fairy lights as they came to a stop outside the entrance; it wasn't Christmas, but with the air December-cold, lights still hung, and Sully next to her, she could just about imagine it. At the door, Sully announced their reservation to a younger-looking woman Lauryn assumed to be the hostess as she surveyed their immediate surroundings. The air hummed with light chatter, booths lining the walls of the restaurant, the floor mostly taken up by smaller tables set for two, four in rarer instances. With the stretch of the bar, there was just enough room for waiters to weave through freely. More than clustered though, the set up and low lights projected intimacy. The kind of place for close friends, or a date.

They followed as a waiter led them toward the rear of the restaurant, Sully whispering how she'd requested a corner booth in the back "Just in case."

Just in case what? Someone recognized Lauryn? Somehow, she didn't think this was the kind of place she'd run into any rabid fans.

About halfway to their table, she caught sight of a head of raven hair that demanded a closer look—perfectly straight, carefully leveled against the back of a red, silk blouse. Her steps slowed, gaze narrowing as if to see clearer in the dimness. And then the woman looked up, her profile on full display—the delicate curve of her jaw and plump lips, radiance of her umber complexion beneath the orange glow of a nearby hanging light.

Mia.

"Here we are," announced the hostess.

Lauryn refocused with a gulp and smiled a thank you.

"Someone will be right over to take your orders."

Her gaze wandered across the room again at Mia's laugh, her whole body attuned to the presence of her. They'd only spoken once since the showing, that same afternoon when Mia had called to ask if Lauryn would be available to see another unit the following Wednesday, with the possibility of one more to follow the same day. She hadn't mentioned their argument or Lauryn's mini meltdown, had kept her tone all business all three minutes of their conversation, except for those last ten seconds when her tone had softened almost imperceptibly as she asked, "Did you...make it back to the office to get your car okay?"

Lauryn relayed that she had.

Mia hung up with a terse. "Okay then."

Looking at her now, that call felt like forever ago. Mia, a stranger. Lauryn, a powerless admirer.

"Someone you know, kiddo?"

Lauryn cleared her throat, fixing her gaze on Sully. "Yeah. Sort of."

Sully's brows inched up. "Going to say more or just leave an old lady wondering?"

A gentle laugh escaped Lauryn's lungs. "Five minutes ago, you were as young as you feel."

"Now I'm as old as I feel." Sully laced the fingers of her hands together, dropped them on the table and hunched forward as if this was the best bit of gossip she'd heard all week. "So?"

"She's my realtor, Sul."

"Realtor? Who knew Denver was so popular for Angelenos this time of year." Sully reached for her menu. "Wanna go say hello?"

Again, Lauryn glanced at Mia. She nearly considered it —going over, saying hi. The woman seated opposite Mia smiled bashfully, pushing a few strands of wavy blonde hair out of her face before resting a hand on Mia's forearm. Lauryn ignored the clench in her stomach, grabbing her own menu as she mumbled, "No. That looks...private. Besides, she's not from LA. She's a co-owner at Flippin' Fantastic."

Sully paused the scan of her menu, frowning. "Isn't that just downtown?"

"Yup." Lauryn grinned. "I'm buying a new place. Here."

"Get out." The veil over Sully's smile rose tentatively.

Lauryn held her stare.

"Get out!"

She cracked, laughing as Sully's excitement flooded her veins—pure, sincere euphoria.

"Lo, why didn't you say anything?"

Lauryn shrugged. "Wanted it to be a surprise, I guess. It was kind of spur of the moment, too. I needed to be sure before I told you."

"So, it's settled? Where is it?"

"Well, it's not *that* settled. We're still looking." But yes, even after two decidedly bad meetings and fifty minutes with her therapist Jacqueline, Lauryn was sure. There were things she wanted in her life, things she wanted to hold on to and never let go. Sully was one of them. Sully was the person who saw something in her when no one else had, not her own parents, not the eleven families she'd passed through, not any of her other teachers. Who said you can't choose your family?

Sully's eyes welled with tears. "Lo..."

Lauryn smiled, blinking away the sting in her own eyes. "You're getting soft on me, Sul."

"Oh, you always knew I was a big ball of feelings. It's what got me drinking in the first place," Sully joked.

"Sul."

"You two about ready to order?"

Lauryn looked up as an androgynous-leaning waiter stopped by their table. "Um." She'd barely even skimmed the first page of the menu. "How's your Agedashi?"

"Best in the city." The waiter beamed.

"That's what I've been telling her," Sully mumbled.

Lauryn laughed, resting her menu on the table. "You know what? The reigns are yours, oh wise one. I'll have whatever she says for all my courses."

Sully rubbed her hands together in excitement. "Okay." Lauryn listened as Sully scanned the menu, muttering a few dishes aloud and conferring with the waiter every now and then, the smile on both their faces constant, the waiter obviously amused too. An instinct prickled at her senses, though —that feeling of being watched twisting up her spine—and she looked up reluctantly. Her eyes locked with Mia's and the beat of her heart faltered then doubled, but she steadied her gaze, and she grounded herself in her booth, in the sound of Sully and the waiter's exchange. What the hell was so funny anyway?

Mia licked her lips, dropped her gaze and faced her date.

"Okay, Sully. I'll be right back with those drinks."

Lauryn blinked. When had they exchanged names?

Sully glanced from Lauryn to where Mia sat across the room then back. "You know, Lo."

Lauryn sighed. *Here we go.*

"We meet thousands of people in a lifetime. Some we remember, some we don't, but something in us always shifts with the special ones." Sully shook her head. "We can't always help it. I know I couldn't. With the way you've been looking at that realtor, I'd say you can't help it either."

"Sul..." Lauryn clenched her jaw. She didn't want to lie to Sully. She'd never been any good at it, but she didn't want to admit to this idea of Mia being special either. She was. Of course, she was. Lauryn felt it in all her senses. But it was so absurd. She'd met Mia, what, a week ago? How special could she be? They could barely make it an hour without an argument.

Sully smiled, leaning forward to whisper, "Wasn't just you looking, kid."

CHAPTER 9

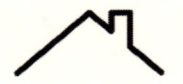

Mia sat on one of the benches outside Flippin' Fantastic, skimming through emails as Darby detailed the surprise she'd planned for Astrid over their daily call. "It's a great idea, Darbs. I'm sure Astrid is going to love it."

"I hope so. I promised *a lot* of babysitting in exchange for borrowing that VR headset."

"You're using your connections." Mia's gaze shifted to the time—2:21—then back to the open email on the screen of her phone. "Besides, you wouldn't be doing all this if you didn't think she was worth it."

"We're all worth it, M."

Mia playfully rolled her eyes. "Sure, babe."

Darby's ability to see the good in practically anyone was one of Mia's favorite things about her. She could always count on Darby for a healthy dose of positivity whenever she needed it, but it was safe to say their friendship hadn't made Mia any less cynical, especially in the last six months. Besides, she'd known Darby long enough to appreciate that all that sunshine had fought through its fair share of clouds over the years.

In the periphery of her gaze, a black SUV rolled to a stop by the curb and one heavily tinted window gave way to Lauryn behind the wheel. "Listen, Darbs, I've got to go. My client's here."

"Oh, if it's the Davidsons, tell Rachel I finally rebuilt that Eiffel Tower Lego set their daughter smashed in my office, and it's really okay. Arty helped me find all the pieces and everything."

"It's not Mrs. Davidson. We closed last week, actually." Mia started toward the car, contemplating leaving her answer at that then deciding not elaborating would give things between her and Lauryn a power she didn't want it to have. "It's Lauryn. I'm taking her to see the four-bedroom in Platt Park then maybe one more unit after that?" she asked more than stated. Last week's showing had taken up special residence in her mind—especially the look on Lauryn's face when Mia had mentioned her parents. Mia's stomach churned. Things between her and Lauryn were going spectacularly not well, and she was unsure what today would hold.

"I love that house!"

Mia smiled, pausing with one hand on the handle of the car door. "You love all the houses. Let's all do patio night at James' later?"

"Yes. We need to settle on what color binoculars case we should get Zee."

"Of course. First order of business. Later, babe." Mia hung up, opened the door and slipped into the passenger's seat. A subtle mélange of smells engulfed her—vanilla and the faintest undertone of something she couldn't pin down—and her eyes drifted to Lauryn. Her curly dark hair sat in a messy puff atop her head, leaving a few loose curls to dangle against her neck and forehead. Mia had never been one for hoodies beyond the threshold of her own front door —and okay, maybe James and Darby's—but the heavy-blend Lauryn wore looked cashmere-soft and exceedingly comfortable.

"Hey," Lauryn greeted softly.

Mia locked eyes with her. "How was your weekend?" She was used to making small talk with clients, but somehow the question felt forced.

"Good. Yours?"

"Good."

Lauryn nodded. "Great. Should we..." She pointed to the computerized dashboard of the SUV, and Mia's brows drew closer in question. "Put in the address?" Lauryn clarified.

"Oh. Right. Yes." Mia reached forward and tapped the darkened monitor. She had been perfectly ready to mumble *turn right here, take this left* the whole ride over, but of course putting it in the GPS would make more sense. There was no reason for all the mindless small talk. Except, in any other instance there would be. She'd ask about partners and kids, jobs, if they'd caught the last Broncos game although she totally didn't have the patience for football on a personal level. Then, she'd take the jumble of information she'd garnered and narrow her showings to the perfect school district, queer neighborhood, even more racially diverse suburb. Real estate was a fine art, and Lauryn's reservation had left Mia painting with dollar store brushes. Or was it Mia's personal grudge that had been keeping her from doing her job? She leaned back in her seat and secured her seatbelt, reluctant to give it more thought.

Lauryn's eyes followed her every move, and her hand tingled with the compulsive urge to tap open her camera app and double check she wasn't sporting a lipstick smudge. She took out her AirPods partly to busy her hands with something else, but mostly because wearing them everywhere was a level of obnoxious she refused to attain. They didn't accessorize well anyway.

The buildings and people blurred together as they drove in silence, Lauryn humming along to songs streaming through the speakers. Coffee shop music. Far cry from the party hits she'd churned out on her last album. It had hit number two on the charts though, which happened to be on the list of useless facts Mia had stumbled on in her three-day obsessive slump, and not the fact that Lauryn had been raised in foster care. Guess "no parents" didn't make for a sexy story. Mia found herself drawn to Lauryn's profile again —the cut of her jaw, subtle movement of her lips—and she wondered about that older woman Lauryn had been with at the restaurant on Friday night, if she was part of the family Lauryn had mentioned. "Was that the first time you'd been to Sushi Den?" It came out before she'd even really thought about it.

"Uh"—Lauryn glanced at her before facing the road again—"Yeah."

A moment passed, Lauv's "Love Somebody" starting up.

"Guessing it wasn't your first time," she said. "At the restaurant, I mean."

Mia shook her head. "I'm kind of obsessed with their wasabi sashimi, but I was actually only there for a client meeting the other night."

"Oh," Lauryn murmured.

Mia waited for more words to follow. Lauryn kept her gaze steady but shifted slightly in her seat. "What?" Mia asked.

"Nothing." Lauryn shrugged. "I don't know. I guess it kind of looked like a date."

Mia's forehead creased as her mind went over the details

of the night. Like Lauryn, their client, Sierra Brooklyn, was a recent courtship. She had been a little...touchy for someone Mia had just met, but some people genuinely had a poor appreciation of personal space, and Mia wasn't triggered by a few brushes of her arm and lingering looks. *Wait...* Her frown deepened. Had she been so out of the dating loop she'd forgotten what flirting looked like? Now that she thought about it, Sierra's "call me" at the end of dinner sounded more like an invitation to tour *her* unit than for Mia to show one of Flippin' Fantastic's. "That was *not* a date."

"It wasn't?" This time, Lauryn looked at her a little longer.

Mia held her gaze, wondering at the thoughts behind her eyes. What did it matter if it'd been a date? How was it any of Lauryn's business? She parted her lips to ask as much, but the words that came out were, "It wasn't."

A buzz stirred up in her lap, and she startled.

Lauryn mumbled, "Yours?"

"Yeah." Mia nodded, reaching into her tote to find her phone nestled next to her tablet, the screen alight with her brother's name. Her eyes drifted to the time though she had a pretty good idea based on her arrangements with Lauryn to meet at 2:30. He never called in the middle of the day like this—not when he knew how likely it was she'd be with a client. "Sorry. I need to take this."

"Yeah. Of course."

Mia swiped her thumb over the green button and brought the phone to her ear. "Matt?"

"Layla passed out at work," he rushed out.

"What? Is she okay?"

"Think so. She's conscious, but a coworker took her to

the ER to get checked out. Can you get Bella and Zac from school? I can't get to the sitter."

"Matt, I'm with a client."

"Shit. Okay. Uh…" A car beeped and unlocked in the background. "Let me call mom and dad."

Mia sighed. "That's an hour-long drive." Their dad rarely got behind the wheel anymore, preferring not to once he'd hit sixty-five and his vision and patience had started a steady decline. Mom had never liked it in the first place.

"Mia, is everything okay?" Lauryn asked.

Matt rambled on. "I mean, I guess I could try to go get them first and take them with me to the ho—"

"No," Mia cut him off. She tugged her bottom lip between her teeth, thinking it over for a second. She was on the verge of losing this contract anyway. "Go make sure Layla's okay. I'll get them."

"But what about your—"

"Matt," she interjected firmly. "Go make sure your wife's okay."

Matt released an audible breath. "Thanks, Mi. I love you."

"I love you, too. Don't speed. And call me when you can."

"I will."

The call disconnected with a beep, and Mia registered the car coming to a stop as Lauryn pulled over. "I'm really sorry to have to do this, Lauryn, but I have to go. Family emergency."

"Okay." Lauryn leaned closer, confusion and concern all etched into her features. "Where do you need to be? I can take you."

Mia shook her head, fingers swift across the screen of her phone. "No. I'll just order a Lyft." A soft hand adorned with a pair of mismatched rings halted her movement. Her heartbeat stopped then kicked into a sprint. Panic. Worry over Layla, she told herself. When she locked eyes with Lauryn again, she expected Lauryn to withdraw her hand, but the pressure of it increased subtly instead.

"I'm not just going to let you out on the side of the street, Mia, so please tell me where you need to be."

"Um…" Mia blinked, her gaze roaming Lauryn's face, trying to make sense of the moment. But this was hardly the time. "I need to get my niece and nephew from school."

"School. Okay. I can do school." Lauryn retracted her hand and shifted into drive.

MIA TOOK PRUDENTLY short strides as she neared the exit of Brayland Academy, Bella on one arm and Isaac on the other. His little feet were nearing running pace, but after the third time she'd attempted to carry him and he'd fussed his way back to the ground, she'd decided to let him have his independence. Good for him, and her Belluno belted jacket. He was endlessly adorable, but drool marks in public did not appeal to her peace of mind. Then again, neither did the straps of the two backpacks digging into her shoulders. "What do you have in here, Bells? Rocks?"

Bella giggled, peering up at Mia. "No, silly. I have my tablet, my math book, my science book, my painting set, my journal…"

Mia released Bella's hand to open the door as they got to the exit and held it for Bella to go first, while tightening her grip on Zac. The kid was a runner, and though he probably wouldn't get far with his penchant for falling, the concrete walkway outside the academy would not be as kind to his delicate little hands as the polished cherrywood he was used to at home. Bella, however, had patiently waited for Mia to reclaim her hand before taking another step. "Sweetie, aren't you supposed to leave some of that stuff here?"

"I don't like to leave them. Other kids touch them when I do."

Right. Mia had never been good at letting other people around her stuff either—no one ever put things back in their place or handled them the way they were supposed to —but then she met Darby and James, and Darby happened to be impossible to say no to and James had enough quirks of her own to appreciate Mia's.

Lauryn hopped out of her car and briskly started toward them—hands stuffed in the pockets of her hoody, hips hugged in skintight distressed jeans and a pair of gleaming sneakers on her feet. "Need some help?" She came to a stop a few feet away, and Mia inadvertently breathed her in. Vanilla. Roses?

What. The. Fuck, Mia? She snapped out of her haze, offering an indignant, "I've got it."

Lauryn regarded Bella and Zac, her lips tugging into a smile. "And who are these cuties?"

"Isabella Andrea Harriott-Stone," Bella announced, offering her free hand.

Lauryn chuckled, stooping to get on eye level with her. "Wow."

Okay, so Mia was just supposed to stand there as a bag rack.

"That's a really pretty name." Zac tugged on Lauryn's hoody and she smiled at him, resting a hand on his belly before addressing her more demanding new acquaintance. "I'm Lauryn. It's nice to meet you."

"Are you Aunt Mia's friend, like Darby and James?"

Lauryn glanced up at Mia, and try all she might, Mia couldn't be angry at being made to wait out this undeniably endearing exchange. "Well..." She looked at Bella, lowering her voice to a pitch Mia had almost missed over the buzz of traffic. "I actually don't think Aunt Mia likes me so much, but she *is* helping me find a house."

"You don't have a house?" Bella found the concept completely appalling.

Mia bit down on a smile, rolling her eyes as she said, "You didn't have to stay, you know?"

Lauryn stood and shrugged. "Why wouldn't I stay?"

Better question: why would she? Mia held onto Zac, tugging him back as he busied himself with the exposed bits of Lauryn's thigh and the fraying threads on her jeans. *Note to self: Give Zac the consent talk early.*

"Is that your car?" Bella piped in again. "Aunt Mia, are we going to help you find Lauryn a house?"

"No, sweetie."

"Shit." Lauryn's eyes widened, and Mia wasn't sure if it was because she'd just sworn in front of the kids, or because of what came next. "Sorry." She looked from Bella to Zac then back to Mia. "Should I have gotten, like, car seats?"

"What? No, Lauryn, really, you've done enough, and my house isn't too far from here. What would you even do with them after one use?"

"I don't know. Donate them, I guess."

Mia stared at her, waiting for an *I'm kidding*. She was kidding, right? Who gets car seats to give someone a ride once?

Lauryn reached forward, fingers brushing against Mia's arm as she lifted Bella's bag from her shoulder. "Come on.

It's not like you knew this was going to happen. Clients can help realtors too, right? It's like *Human Decency 101*."

"Lauryn..." Mia parted and closed her lips. Words lingered at the back of her throat to decline Lauryn's help again. What was it her mom always said? She was stubbornly independent. But independence aside, Lauryn was still Lauryn and even with her boxes of sunshine, soft smells and gorgeous eyes, and her inexplicable kindness, thinking about Cori still hurt. Was this how Lauryn had won her over? Or had Cori just looked at her and decided to blow up a year and the promise of a future for one night? "Nothing." Mia forced a smile. "Thank you."

Lauryn's stare lingered, her brows knit as if to decipher a puzzle but then she slung Bella's bag over her own shoulder and mumbled, "Don't mention it."

THE RIDE over to Mia's apartment had taken twice as long— Mia seated in the back with Zac in her lap, Bella buckled in and Lauryn driving below the speed limit as she fielded Bella's two hundred questions.

"Why don't you have a house? Do you want to stay with us? We have six bedrooms. *Six*. I'm sure Aunt Mia will help you though. She's mean sometimes, but Daddy says it's only because she's a *per-func-tionalist*."

"Really?" Lauryn asked through a laugh, her eyes meeting Mia's in the rearview.

"Mhm." Bella gave an exaggerated nod.

Zac babbled his support.

Traitors.

"But she's also really nice. She loves me and Zac, and

Mommy and Daddy, and Darby and James, and sometimes when we watch Frozen, she crie—"

"Okay, Bells, Lauryn needs to focus on driving so we can make it home safely, yeah?"

"But—"

"Safety first, love."

"Don't worry, Bells." Lauryn winked. "You can tell me all about it later."

Later? Who said anything about later?

"Okay, Laurie."

Was that a nickname? Mia furrowed her brows at Bella. Clearly, she needed to put a stop to this now. Lauryn was to take them home, where Mia would promise from the confines of this car to reschedule a day of uninterrupted showings—she would will the fucking universe into complicity. They'd close on a house in a week. Two, tops. Lauryn would never see the kids again, or Mia for that matter. Life would go on. Mia would let Darby create that *Her* profile she'd been on about for weeks. Maybe. Unlikely.

The second they'd pulled into Mia's garage and gotten out of the car, her carefully thought-out plan had begun to crumble.

"Laurie," Bella sung, swinging their joined hands. "Will you help me with my homework?"

"Uh..." Lauryn glanced at Mia, clearing her throat. "I think I have to go now, Bells."

Mia's mind raced with the phrasing of Lauryn's answer. Did she not *want* to go now?

Zac shifted in Mia's arms, patting her cheeks with both hands. "Mi-mi."

The look of pure adoration in Lauryn's eyes left her flustered and indecisive. Two things she did not like to be.

"Aunt Mia, can Lauryn please stay?" Bella pleaded. "Just for a little while."

No. Why couldn't Mia just come out and say it? No. Lauryn could not stay, because it was *Lauryn* and this was Mia's home, and today had been so weird on so many levels.

"Hey." Lauryn stooped to Bella's height, brushing a hand over her cheek. "I'm going to walk with you to the door, but then I have to go."

"But Laurie—"

"Aunt Mia is going to help you with your homework, and you're going to get an A." She scrunched her nose, pressing her forehead to Bella's and Bella spurred into a soft giggle. "A plus."

Warmth spread in Mia's chest.

"So, you're not going to give her a hard time, right?"

"No."

"Good." Lauryn raised her hand for a high five, but Bella wrapped her hands around her neck, almost knocking her to the floor. She caught her bearings quickly and returned the hug.

Mia gulped, looking away. "Okay. Let's get inside."

They rode the elevator to the sixth floor in silence, Zac's clapping and jabbering being the exception. Apparently, Bella had mentioned "Laurie" enough for him to take the new nickname for a spin too, though he may have been having a little trouble with his Ls. Lauryn didn't seem to mind—she'd been perfectly at ease with Bella's hand in hers and periodically making faces that left Zac squirming with laughter in Mia's arms. She'd definitely need to have a talk with Matt and Layla about how their children had bonded with an enemy of the family in no more than an hour. Not. Good. To her relief, when they got there, Bella had entered her apartment without a fight and Zac in tow.

Mia lowered her bags to the floor and did a quick visual sweep of the living room to make sure nothing hazardous had been left out.

"They're beautiful."

She turned at Lauryn's soft declaration. "Yeah. They kind of are, aren't they?"

"You going to be okay?" She shut her eyes, shaking her head. "Dumb question. Of course, you will. I hope everything goes well with Layla."

"Me too. Thanks." Mia pulled her bottom lip between her teeth. "He said she was conscious. I think the ER's just a precaution."

Lauryn nodded, sliding her hands into the pockets of her hoody. "Mia—"

"Laur—"

She breathed a laugh. "You go."

Mia's chest tightened. "I just...I'm really sorry about all this. Everything else aside, I feel like ever since you walked into my office last week, all you've seen are things I try to keep out of my professional life and none of the things that made Drew refer me in the first place."

"Mia, nothing I've seen today has changed my mind about you. If anything, I want to work with you even more."

It didn't make sense. Not Lauryn's words. Not any of this.

Behind them, Zac squealed, and Bella yelled, "Isaac!"

Lauryn's eyes lit up with a smile as she tried to look past Mia. "You should probably go take care of that."

"Yeah," she mumbled, checking to make sure Bella and Zac weren't about to maim each other, or themselves. And she didn't know why, but when she faced Lauryn again, Lauryn muttering faint words about how meeting had been nice, even if they hadn't made it to the house and how she'd be happy to reschedule, Mia stepped closer—too close—and cut her off with a touch on her arm. "Lauryn..."

She cast a furtive glance at Mia's hand then met her gaze. "Mia?"

"Stay. For Bella and Zac. And maybe we'll actually get somewhere with what you're looking for in a house."

"Yeah?"

Mia nodded. "Yes."

CHAPTER 10

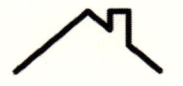

Lauryn watched from her car as Mia and her brother, Matt, talked by the front door of his house. Her exchange with him—a rushed and barely audible introduction from Mia—had been characterized by ten seconds of polite smiling, a quick thank you and a side-eye Lauryn had pretended to not see him shoot his sister. She'd never gotten close to any of her siblings in the dozen homes she'd passed through, but she knew better than to attempt to decipher an unspoken secret between brother and sister.

The sun had gone into hiding more than an hour ago, and the cold descended right on time. An elderly couple strolled by chattering softly, but the neighborhood was otherwise still beneath the darkened sky. Nice houses ranging from traditional to modern architecture—the kind of houses Lauryn could only dream of not too long ago. It helped to know she wouldn't be the only person of color for miles if she decided to live here. Denver was no LA, although she had read that Hispanics and Latinos accounted for a noteworthy percent of the population. Was that the kind of thing Mia would be happy to know she'd spent the weekend considering? What she'd like in a neighborhood. She'd probably be relieved to know Lauryn had contemplated it at all. Not that they had gotten a chance to talk about it with Bella monopolizing two thirds of their time, and Isaac the rest. It was still baffling how the toddler was more low maintenance, or was it, considering Bella had clearly taken after a particular someone?

Mia's apartment was exactly how Lauryn imagined. Modern-chic. Floor to ceiling windows and gleaming appliances. Shades of white accented with a blue throw and caramel wingback chair. Nothing out of place, probably not so kid friendly. It was a mess by the time Matt had called to say he and Layla were home. Something told Lauryn Bella and Zac were the only people who could ever get away with it.

The passenger side door opened, and she turned as Mia slipped in. "All set?"

"Yeah." Mia dropped her head against the headrest and faced Lauryn.

In another time, Lauryn would reach up and stroke her cheek, get lost in the deep brown of her eyes, kiss her slowly, relish the touch and taste of her lips, especially with the way Mia was looking at her now.

"Thanks for waiting. I'm really starting to regret leaving my car at the office today."

Tonight, Lauryn was drunk on the domesticity of a day buffered by lovely kids and too many emotions, and kissing her realtor would be a very bad idea. "I could drive you back there instead if you want."

"No. Thank you, but no, Lauryn."

"Okay."

"Actually"—she sat upright, brows drawn together as if a spark had gone off inside her head. "One of the houses I wanted to show you is right around here. Do you, and you can totally say no considering you spent all our scheduled time helping me babysit, but do you want to go see it?"

Lauryn smiled. "Do you always do showings after office hours?"

"Not always, but I do feel like you've earned an exception."

She hadn't been trying to earn anything. Not consciously anyway. She'd been in Hollywood long enough to know some things, some people, inspired the worst in her—her escapism, insecurity, reservation—and with others, all her best traits would erupt like a dormant volcano. She could try to fight it, but defying gravity might be simpler.

"You don't have to, of course," Mia added. "If you have somewhere to be or don't feel up to it right now."

"I don't have anywhere to be. I've been here, what, fourteen nights? More than half have been spent with my guitar, ineffectively working on my next album, and the others hanging out with Sully and her wife."

"Is that the woman you were with the other night?"

Lauryn bobbed her head in agreement, willing herself to not get stuck on the moment they'd shared—Mia's eyes locked on hers, the race of her heart, Sully's insinuation that Mia was special. "She's my self-proclaimed godmother, part of who I meant when I mentioned family, I guess."

Mia settled against her headrest again, facing Lauryn like she'd done before. "Who else?"

Lauryn mirrored her position. "Blake, Drew's girlfriend. Drew, too, although we never were as close. My manager, Ken. He's a little shit and we never agree on my music, but we care about each other in our own way."

"Are they who you meant that night? When you said,

'Somewhere that feels like the place family comes home to'?"

Good memory, Lauryn thought. "In a way, yeah. But I think a part of me meant my own family, you know? The one I'll have someday."

"Yeah. I do know." Mia nodded. Her gaze drifted to her lap and when she looked up again, she seemed hesitant. "Lauryn..."

"What happened to them? My bio parents?"

Mia grimaced. "You don't have to answer that."

Lauryn peeked up at the cloudy evening sky. "I don't know." She turned to Mia again. "Never met them. A few years ago, I tried to find out, got a whole team on it, did one of those weird ancestry tests." She scoffed. "All I learned was that I'd been left at a church in Echo Park when I was probably a month old, no paper trail, and apparently that I'm somewhere between 57% Latinx, 39% Black and 4%"—she emphasized with air quotes—"*other races.*"

"Wow." It was barely a whisper. "Lauryn, I..."

Lauryn smiled wistfully. "Yeah." She wasn't sure why she'd told Mia any of that, except that Mia had asked, and honesty felt... right? It's not like her background was a secret, but only a handful of people knew all the details. A handful of people close to her, and now her realtor. Which part of the Flippin' Fantastic new customer profile covered abandonment issues again?

"I'm sorry, by the way," said Mia. "About last week."

Lauryn shook her head. "You were just doing your job. I guess some days it just stings more than others. And if I'm being honest, I was kind of pissed at you for what you said earlier." She clenched her jaw. "About falling into my lap. Guessing it's because you saw that picture, right?"

Mia visibly tensed.

"That night isn't the sum of me, Mia. I may have been complicit in being there, but I never touched any of those drugs. I don't even know how they got in, except for the obvious fact that people snuck them in. And that girl everyone is so hung up on..."

"Lauryn—"

"I don't even remember her name. All I know is, she'd been there with two other women, all three of them hammered. She stumbled and fell in my lap and I caught her. And I may have been a little drunk too, so when she kissed me, I kissed her back—"

"Lauryn, why are you telling me any of this?" Mia gritted out. Total 180 from the sincere tone and affection of a minute ago.

"I..." Lauryn had fucking whiplash. "I don't know, Mia."

Mia sunk her teeth into her bottom lip and shut her eyes, one hand on the handle of her door. "You're right. It is late. Let's just meet again on Friday like we planned."

"Mia."

"I'm sorry." She pushed the door open and exited the car.

"Mia!"

The car tremored when the door slammed. Lauryn sat motionless in her seat, her forehead creased as she watched Mia walk back up the pavement to the front of the house. When Matthieu appeared in the doorway, and Mia stepped inside, Lauryn scoffed, nodding.

So much for fucking special.

"So, to reiterate what you've said, you and Mia, the realtor, had a wonderful afternoon with her niece and nephew, who from the sound of it, you bonded with very quickly." Jacqueline peered down at something off camera—likely that binder she had every session—then adjusted her glasses on the bridge of her nose. "And after this talk in your car about your family and the party incident, she left?"

Lauryn tried to limit the indignance in her tone. Really, it was Mia she was mad at, it was Mia she'd trusted, but she was not in the mood for her therapist's slow repetitions and round-a-bout tactics today. "Yes."

"Are you angry?"

Lauryn breathed an exasperated sigh. "Yes, I'm angry. Wouldn't you be?"

"Possibly."

"And it's the way she left!" Lauryn spit out, sitting up straighter on the sofa of her townhouse. "Like *I* did something wrong, like even after everything, all she can see are those stories."

"Is that why you told her? Because you wanted her to see you as someone else?"

"I don't know. I—It felt right." She shrugged. "We were talking, and she asked about my family, and it seemed like she wanted to know, like genuinely wanted to know, and yes, maybe I wanted her to see me for me. Not the songs I'm forced to sing, or a party from six months ago. Me."

"And who are you, Lauryn?"

Lauryn's gaze went to the empty space on the wall across the room. A gulp slid down her throat. Weeks of Jacqueline asking her that question, affirming how important working on it was to Lauryn's process, and the only thought her brain could muster was, *Who the fuck even knows?*

"Let's come back to it." Jacqueline scribbled a note. "You said you met Mia at a party on New Year's Eve."

"Met is probably making too much of it. We collided in

the entryway, which went well enough until she recognized me. Then she just...stormed off, I guess."

"Seems like you've been colliding ever since. Even if it's not always physical. Your first meeting at her office, the showing a week ago, last night."

Lauryn shrugged. "I guess you could say that."

"Why not get another realtor?"

"Drew recommended her."

"But it's not going well, is it?" Jacqueline paused. "You've seen one house you didn't like and had to cancel two meetings already, all due to her."

"She had a family emergency."

"And your first meeting? I believe you said..." She glanced down at the binder again. "She was *'kind of an asshole'*."

Lauryn huffed. "She was!"

"But the next day you brought her a gift?"

"She had a bad day. She seemed...sad? I felt bad for her."

"You felt bad for her?"

"Yes," Lauryn answered firmly, her tone like her emotions—up and down and all over the place. "Can you stop? Stop doing that thing where you repeat everything I say until I come to the conclusion you've already drawn."

"You're agitated."

No shit.

Jacqueline inhaled a slow breath. "Lauryn...Is it possible that the reason you've given Mia so many chances isn't because Drew recommended her, or even because you're attracted to her, but because she reminds you of someone?"

Lauryn's mind latched onto the words, her heartbeat steady but building almost as if her subconscious had already begun to decipher what Jacqueline meant.

"The anger, the sadness, being so overcome by it she

isolates instead of communicates," Jacqueline went on. "There seem to be some parallels here, Lauryn, between the patience, kindness even, that you've shown Mia and how your relationship with Sully began. The benevolent music teacher and temperamental pupil."

No one had given her as many chances as Sully. Sully was the only reason she'd even made it out of high school. Kids talked a lot of dumb shit and they had a lot to say about the queer, brown girl with no parents and no friends. Back then, Lauryn's answers to all her problems ended with bruised knuckles, but she'd always spent a little too much time in the music room after school. Sully taught her to channel everything she felt into lyrics and instruments.

"Of course, things with Mia have an irrefutably romantic dimension, though you assert she's only your realtor."

"She *is* only my realtor."

"Lauryn..." Jacqueline held her gaze, her tone softer even never being anything but neutral. "Is it possible that you feel so connected to Mia because she reminds you of...you?"

CHAPTER 11

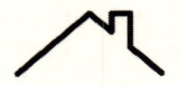

Mia pulled into the driveway behind James and Darby's cars. It'd never failed to amaze her how efficiently what they drove summed up their personalities—a garnet BMW, a red Beetle with a rainbow decal in the back windshield and a well looked after vintage pickup. They were living proof that friendships didn't always have to be defined by similarities, or differences for that matter. She wouldn't trade Darby's persistent bright side or James' strong will for anything, and she needed to see them before heading to the office this morning.

Yesterday, she'd busied herself with back-to-back showings and their pickiest client, Mrs. Giodani, and had almost managed to not think about Lauryn all day. Almost. But the second she'd gotten home her mind had begun to dredge up images of Lauryn in her apartment.

Reading with Bella.

Crawl-chasing Zac through the living room only to playfully bite at his tummy when she did catch him. Mia hadn't seen him laugh like that in... well, ever.

She'd felt herself slipping, gradually becoming more attuned to the flecks of gold in Lauryn's eyes, the smell and feel of her skin, sound of her laugh. It was unfair how good she was with the kids, how good she was with Mia. And maybe for a moment, especially in her car after they'd taken Bella and Zac home, Mia wanted to forget. She *had* forgotten. She wanted nothing more than to spend all night listening to Lauryn and staring into her eyes and wondering just what it was like to taste her lips.

Then she brought up the party, Cori, and Mia just... couldn't.

She dragged in a breath, reaching for the box of pastries and drinks carrier in the passenger seat. The neighborhood was still; the sun struggling to peek out behind a few clouds, but conveniently, neither she, James, nor Darby had ever had trouble starting their days early. Darby tended to overextend, James obsessed over literally every detail, Mia needed *perfect*, and it was a match made in house flipping heaven. As she strutted up the walkway, her eyes drifted to Zee's yard. No binoculars or retreating head behind the hedges in sight.

Thank you powers of James Dean.

The door swung open and Darby stepped out, beaming. Her lips parted then shut as her eyes locked on the box in Mia's hand. "You went to Eleni's?" She frowned. "I would've baked if I knew we had a breakfast date."

Mia smiled, closing the distance to peck her on the cheek. "*I* didn't even know we had a breakfast date. Besides, restaurants do exist for a reason, Darbs."

"Well, are they gluten-free?" Darby asked, walking Mia into the house.

"Mhm." It reeked of saw dust and paint but knocking

down that wall between the living and dining room had really opened up the space, and Mia was already in love with this place, even if it had been costing them a ridiculous amount of time and money. "James, put down the power tools and come have breakfast with us!"

There was a bang, clank, swear then silence. She'd heard.

"And organic?" Darby continued her pastry-probe.

"Of course, babe." Mia lowered the box to a dusty island counter and handed the largest coffee cup to Darby. "Extra sweet. And for James—"

"Here as summoned." James stepped into the room, flipping bangs out of her face as she brushed something off the sleeve of her flannel.

Mia plucked the mid-sized cup out of the holder and offered it. "All the cream Miller Farm could supply."

"Ha ha." James took a slow sip of her coffee.

Mia flipped open the box and took out a strawberry galette, reminding herself to not lean against the counter. White blazers and houses they were actively flipping did not get along—she'd been too distracted while getting dressed this morning to consider that. "Please tell me we've had a morning free of incidents."

"Well," Darby piped in, "The flooring came yesterday and there seems to have been some kind of mix up."

"Mix up?"

James took a step toward the box. "They sent linoleum instead of hardwood."

Mia's eyes widened.

"I'm making it work though."

"Darbs." Mia stared at her. "This isn't the sixties. I can't sell a house with linoleum floors."

"Of course, you can. You can sell anything."

"J..."

James held up a hand with a glazed donut. "I'm not touching this one."

"It'll be cute, I promise. The vision is only..." Darby trailed off, pushing her curly brown hair behind one ear. "Mildly different."

Mia mulled over the words. If Darby had a vision in mind, Mia had no doubt the execution would be absolutely beautiful. Plus, linoleum designs had come a long way in fifty years, but the multi-colored eye sores popping up in her head were anxiety-inducing.

Darby smiled. "It's going to be perfect, M."

Perfect. Mia wouldn't argue with that.

"So, what's going on, M?" James brushed the corner of her lips with a napkin.

Mia's phone buzzed in her pocket and she reached for it, welcoming the opportunity to not look her friends in the eyes right now. "What do you mean?" She scanned the text from Arty—Lauryn had called the office, no message left. Had Lauryn changed her mind about their meeting this morning? Mia glimpsed the time. They'd promised to meet in an hour but cancelling didn't sound so bad. Preferably indefinitely.

"I mean, you showing up with breakfast is pretty much a 911."

Mia looked up with furrowed brows. "It is not."

"Is too, babe," Darby countered.

"How's stuff going with Lauryn?"

"Who said anything about Lauryn?"

James folded her arms across her chest and Darby bobbed her head, singing, "The lady doth protest too much."

Mia huffed, rolling her eyes. "Okay. I'm a mess. Everything's a mess and also, like, super confusing right now. I have no idea what she wants, and I think maybe she was trying to tell me on Wednesday but then she mentioned Cori and I..." She sighed.

"Are we talking about houses or?"

"This does sound suspiciously *not* about houses, M."

It *was* about houses. At least Mia wanted it to be. How the fuck had she even allowed this to happen? Lauryn Matthews of all people. Her phone buzzed again, more incessantly, and she glanced down to see the screen lit up with Lauryn's name. Would sending her to voicemail be unprofessional?

Yes.

Absolutely.

Why was Mia being so weird anyway? For all she knew Lauryn *was* calling to cancel. Mia wouldn't blame her—there had been an undeniable vulnerability between them in her car the other night, Lauryn telling Mia about her family. Mia understood all the more what she'd come searching for in Denver, and she kind of hated herself for leaving the way she did. It's just... There were still so many unresolved feelings about Cori, and Lauryn had all but confirmed that Cori had been the one to initiate their encounter. Drunk or not, Mia couldn't escape the ache hearing that had unearthed in her chest. Although, it occurred to her that the reason she was upset had been complicated all the more by the fact that Lauryn was the kind of person to just kiss a random stranger who'd fallen into her lap. Wasn't that exactly what she'd thought though?

Her phone stopped ringing then the buzzing started up again.

James stepped closer. "Are you going to get that?"

"Um..."

"Wait, is that her?" Darby's eyes lit up and she snatched the phone out of Mia's hand and brought it to her own ear. "Mia's phone."

"Darby," Mia gritted out, lunging at her.

Darby turned her back to Mia, twisting to keep the phone out of reach. "Oh. Hi, Lauryn. Yeah. This is Darby. Designer third of the Flippin' Fantastic trio."

Mia's heart rattled in her chest.

"No. James and I have been really looking forward to meeting you."

James' forehead creased. "We have?"

Darby laughed, presumably at something Lauryn had said, and Mia rolled her eyes as she went on, "We're actually at one of the houses we're flipping."

"Darby..."

"It's beautiful chaos over here, but you should totally drop by. Then you and M can drive over to your showing."

Mia was going to kill her.

"Okay! Perfect. I'll send you the address." She tapped out a message—dropped a pin, maybe—and spun toward them, face bright with a grin. If it wasn't for the fact that Mia loved her so much and knew she totally meant well, James would have to help Mia fake a construction accident to cover up a murder.

"What the hell, Darbs?" Mia grabbed her phone back and swiped to the call log as if to bolster the idea it had really been Lauryn who'd called. Lauryn's name headed the list with taunting clarity.

"Conflict resolution requires open communication, M. It's not like you were going to ask her to come over."

"The conflict is that she fucked my fiancé. What's there to resolve?"

"M..." James said cautiously. "You said Cori denied anything but a kiss."

"Well, forgive me if I don't put too much stock in what Cori's says happened, James."

Mia remembered that night with painful lucidity—she'd relived it enough in the days after the video had been leaked—and maybe nothing in it had suggested more than a kiss, but she'd called Cori at least half a dozen times and hadn't been able to reach her. By the time she'd called Mia back, it was nearly 1 p.m. the day after. What was Mia supposed to think? It's not like she didn't know who Cori was—how Cori lived and breathed being the center of attention, the person who could walk into a room and have anyone she wanted. Wasn't that why she'd gone after Mia in the first place? Because at least on the outside, everything about Mia screamed unapproachable, ice queen, conquest.

Well, Cori had come, saw and fucking conquered. Mia owed it to herself to never go there again, so she was content with believing the worst.

Darby placed an arm on Mia's shoulder. "I don't think James said that for Cori's benefit, babe."

Mia sighed.

"What did you mean? About Lauryn and things being confusing?"

"I don't know," her voice quaked as she looked from Darby to James. "I hate her, but I also don't? Because I think...I think nothing I know about her is true. I think she's a good person, like a really kind person, and it's scary because the more I'm around her, the more I want to be? I've been telling myself I don't because it would be so much easier if it were true."

She licked her lips, and all she wanted was the simple

comfort of her bed, a tub of strawberry Haagen Dazs and Killing Eve reruns.

"I don't even think she knows about Cori. Two nights ago, she basically tried to explain that the woman in the picture didn't mean anything, and maybe she was doing that because she felt it...this bubble we'd been trapped in all day where nothing existed but me and her and Bella and Zac, and there was something so idyllic about it. I'm pretty sure if she'd kissed me, I would've kissed her back. But she didn't and the woman in the picture isn't no one, and I don't know what to do about any of this."

"Shit," James breathed. "So, this was an actual 911, then."

Mia laughed and Darby pouted, moving closer to wrap her arms around Mia's neck. "Maybe I should call her back and cancel."

The second the words left Darby's lips, raps echoed from the front door.

Mia prayed to the house flipping gods it was Zee coming over to finally say thank you for her new binoculars case.

LAURYN STOOD by the front door, eyes roaming the entryway of the house as she fidgeted with the tapered sleeves of her oatmeal turtleneck. Like two days ago, she'd paired her sweater with skintight black jeans but had traded her sneakers for heeled booties. Her curly dark hair, full-bodied and free of her typical high puff, brushed her shoulder with every turn of her head and Mia was grateful for all the walls she'd built around herself. Because the last time she'd felt this weight in her chest, she'd closed her eyes to a hundred red flags and bought a ring.

She took a step forward, into the bubble of rose vanilla

emanating from Lauryn and dug deep for all her proficiency. "So, this actually wasn't supposed to be on the list of showings. At least, not yet."

Lauryn's gaze fell to hers and held, fire and gold and questions burning in her eyes.

An apology lingered on Mia's tongue—sorry for the way she left the other night, sorry she's been such a raging bitch at times, sorry she...just... sorry. But she could feel Darby in the background waiting for an intro and James set for an escape, and this wasn't the time to say any of it.

"Well, it turns out I was close by and"—Lauryn looked past Mia and her lips stretched in a smile—"Darby mentioned beautiful chaos, which is kind of every artist's wet dream."

Mia's brows inched up. Nope. Not letting her mind go there.

Darby appeared next to her with an outstretched hand. "I'm Darby. Did you get here okay? I drove right past the house my first time over."

Lauryn breathed a laugh. "Blame the GPS. It's always the GPS' fault."

Mia twisted in her spot to watch the exchange. She couldn't decide if this was betrayal or support. Well, she knew exactly which it was, but still.

From the landing of the stairs, James held up a hand in their direction, "James Dayhuff," then ruffled her bangs, mumbling, "I think I uh...left the hammer on upstairs. Just going to go check on that." She turned, her long legs carrying her six-foot form up the stairs two at a time.

Lauryn frowned.

"Consider it a compliment." Darby rubbed her shoulder, guiding her toward the living room. "She barely talked to

Mia the day they met too and here we are. Best friends and business partners."

"That's some story."

"Right?" Darby nodded, her smile bright enough to power the room. She pushed her glasses up the bridge of her nose. "Do you meditate? I'm getting a really Zen, sort of broody vibe off you."

"Yeah?" Lauryn laughed. "I don't actually, but my therapist has been trying to talk me into it for months."

Mia narrowed her gaze at Lauryn. *She has a therapist?* So did James and Darbs but Lauryn didn't really seem like the therapy type. Then again, what did that even look like?

"I totally recommend. But listen..." Darby trailed off, her gaze shifting to Mia's. "I'm going to go help James check on that hammer and let M show you this gem of a house. When you decide to buy it, we can talk design over lunch."

"Sounds great, Darby." Lauryn's smiled never faltered, and okay, maybe Mia should go check on the hammer and let Darbs do the showing.

She stopped next to Mia on her way out, leaning in to whisper, "You were right. She might be a good egg."

"I can't believe you did this to me."

"Love you too, babe." She squeezed Mia's arm, "You're going to do great," and then she was gone.

Lauryn took a few steps deeper into the room before spinning on the heels of her boots, thumb of one hand hooked into the back pocket of her jeans. "I like them. Your friends."

There was something in the way she'd chosen the word friends instead of business partners that pushed the idea that this meeting was even remotely professional further to the back of Mia's mind. Mia sighed. "They like you, too."

"Try not to sound so disappointed."

"I'm not. They usually have good instincts about who I spend my time with."

"Then I'm glad I passed Darby's aura test. Think she's gone to tell James I'm all right?"

"Maybe." Mia was staring—she knew she was. Denial was a terrible thing, but the admission she'd made mere minutes before Lauryn walked in with her hair framing her cheekbones, her eyes and skin meadowy and warm had left Mia with way too many emotions to sort through and not nearly enough time.

Lauryn broke eye contact and pointed toward the exposed beams of the ceiling. "I like those."

"Me too." Mia stepped closer. "James had them put in last week. She's also having some lights fitted between them for that perfect cozy-night-in effect. Darbs has her going for a modern rustic look. We'll have panoramic doors leading to the backyard, which needs a lot of landscaping, but the great thing is there's so much space to work with and the old owners kept it pretty bare, except for a stage if you can believe it. Anyway, we can do anything from an earthy escape to something more contemporary."

Lauryn's expression softened. "You like it. This house."

"It has good bones. Great potential. But I guess some things you just feel good about, you know?"

"I know what you mean." Her gaze lingered as if trying to decipher Mia's thoughts, in search of some deeper understanding. "Give me the walkthrough."

"Lauryn, we can really just go to the unit I had planned. James does a wonderful job of keeping things organized here but it's still a mess right now. Contractors are going to start showing up any minute."

"Mia," she said softly. "Show me. Please."

Mia tried not to think about the way she'd asked, her

tone beseeching, gaze steady. She tried not to think about the way her own gaze fell to Lauryn's lips when she answered, "Okay."

MIA HAD SPENT NEARLY the entire tour leading an unsettlingly silent Lauryn—the click of her stilettos and tap of Lauryn's boots the only sound between them when Mia wasn't rattling off details about flooring and which rooms came equipped with one of the four fireplaces. Incomplete units were always more difficult. It required a level of imagination clients didn't always possess. Unfurnished, dusty rooms with exposed piping and damaged floors were nothing compared to the glitz of a newly renovated house. Complete units almost always carried most of the weight in a showing, leaving Mia to bear the rest with just the right amount of natural charm and knowledge. Being a realtor was second nature though, and she'd found herself making it through the ground floor and most of the second with practiced ease.

Yet, her mind wandered constantly to Lauryn. Her smell. The way she always seemed to be standing just behind Mia every time they entered a new room. The way she'd jokingly asked James how the hammer was doing when they'd caught up to her and Darby in bathroom number four of six. She thought about last Tuesday at the first apartment. Lauryn's family. Two days ago with Bella and Zac. Later in her car just the two of them. Cori.

They'd made it back downstairs and to the designated media room in the basement, the media room Mia suddenly realized could be a studio instead, when Lauryn turned to look at her and murmured, "This is it."

Mia blinked. "What?"

"The house. This is the one, Mia."

"Wait...Lauryn, there are other units. This won't be finished for at least another three to four weeks."

Lauryn shrugged. "I'm not in a rush. Besides, isn't this usually the aim of these things? To sell the house."

"Yes, but—"

"It's everything I want, Mia. I think it's actually better that it's not finished. I might take Darby up on that lunch date, pick her brain a little more about her ideas."

"Lauryn," Mia breathed. Darby would love that, and she and James would probably kill Mia if they knew Lauryn wanted to buy and she'd so much as suggested otherwise. After all the money they'd poured into it, one ridiculous incident after another, Zee, the neighbor from hell. Then again, James didn't seem to mind the latter anymore.

"This is a good thing, isn't it?" Lauryn asked. "The hard part is over, Mia. Send me the paperwork, I'll have my lawyers look them over. You'll probably never have to see me again."

Mia's brows drew together. "Two days ago, you didn't even know what you wanted."

"I always knew what I wanted. Even if it's not always easy explaining it, especially to someone who clearly has everything she wants."

"What does that even mean, Lauryn?"

Lauryn scoffed. "Should I try to explain so you can leave again?"

Mia swallowed against the tightness in her throat. Maybe she deserved that. Maybe Lauryn had every right to be upset, but so did Mia. Didn't she?

"You think that's the kind of thing I just tell people?"

"Well, why did you tell me? We barely know each other."

"You know why." Lauryn shook her head, taking a step back. "Because you were there, and you felt it. But you're my realtor, right? Not my groupie. You're not going to just swoon and fall into my lap. Point fucking made, Mia."

Mia closed her eyes, shaking her head. What was she even doing here? Lauryn wanted the house. She should be on her phone with Arty right now, making sure he had the paperwork drawn up and ready for signatures. She sunk her teeth into her bottom lip, and she looked Lauryn dead in the eyes. "You will never get it, Lauryn. Because you don't actually have a clue about anything, do you? That woman you take every opportunity to mention was nothing. No one. She was someone to me."

"Mia, what are you talking about?"

"Her name is Cori, and until six months ago, I thought she was going to be my *wife*, Lauryn."

Lauryn took a step forward, lips slightly agape, lines in her forehead. "Mia—I didn't—She never said anything about being engaged. How was I supposed to know? How was I supposed to know any of this?"

That was the worst part. Mia knew Lauryn didn't know. There was every possibility Cori hadn't even thought of, let alone mentioned, Mia. In a lot of ways, the night she clung to with the idea that it had ruined her life was the one that had probably stopped her from making a life-changing mistake. It wasn't that she hadn't seen what her parents and her friends had. But Cori had always been different when she and Mia were alone. They knew each other, loved each other, wanted the same things. At least, Mia thought they did.

"Mia..." Lauryn cradled her face in her hands.

For a minute, she closed her eyes and breathed Lauryn in, allowed herself to dwell in their proximity, and then she backed away, skin burning with traces of Lauryn's touch. "She wasn't no one, Laur." She turned to walk away, but remembering why they were there, paused to look at Lauryn again. "If it's really what you want, this place can be yours in a couple of days. I'll call you when the paperwork is ready."

CHAPTER 12

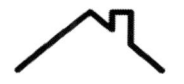

Lauryn stuffed a throw pillow beneath her head as she reclined in the cushioned loveseat on the balcony of her townhouse. At least five hours had gone by since she'd left the house earlier, the house that was to become her home in Denver. Even in its state of disarray, she really had fallen for it. She could imagine nights by a firepit in the backyard, she and Sully talking with steaming cups clutched between their hands. Coffee for Sul. Tea for her. Blake and Drew would visit for weekends. They'd have parties. Friends only.

Hours would be lost in her studio, stringing together the chaos of lyrics her mind dredged up day after day.

She'd finally commit to learning to cook in the beautiful concept of a kitchen. Spend movie nights beneath those exposed beams in the living room with only the light of the screen to go by, and she'd get so distracted by the woman in her arms, they would wind up naked and entwined in front of the fireplace.

And maybe someday, she would fill those rooms with beauties like Bella and Zac, and she could carry, or her wife could, but they would definitely adopt.

Mia's face flashed in her mind, their argument constantly on loop.

Cori. Mia's... fiancé.

Now more than ever, Lauryn would give anything to take that night back, to make sure Mia never had to feel even a fraction of what Lauryn had seen on her face today. And if she couldn't, she would've never set foot in Flippin' Fantastic to begin with.

"Lo." Blake's voice crackled through Lauryn's AirPods, barely carrying over the winds in Point Reyes. Inconvenient for a call, apparently perfect for a perfume ad campaign. "A FaceTime video call usually means some amount of actual face time, you know."

Lauryn sighed, picking up her phone and holding it high enough to capture her face.

A stretch of white sand and cresting waves filled Blake's background, and Lauryn questioned, only for a second, what the fuck had possessed her to leave California in the winter to come house shopping in Denver.

"You have to talk to her," Blake said.

"I wouldn't even know where to start, B. How does anyone get past that? I don't even know why she took the job in the first place."

"I mean, I have a few ideas, but at least now you know why she's been so hot and cold this whole time. Even the run in on New Year's Eve makes sense if you think about it."

"I have thought about it. It's all I can think about."

"She's all you can think about. I've known you, what, eight years? We haven't always been this close, but I have never seen you like this over a girl. Ever. But you have seen me, so I don't need to tell you what it means."

"This is different."

"This is exactly how it started, and I don't think you should ignore it."

"You and Drew are meant for each other. Mia thinks I..." Lauryn scoffed. "I can only imagine what she thinks happened between me and Cori." They all thought the worst. One picture and Lauryn was a womanizing, drug-fiend.

"So, tell her what happened, Lo."

Lauryn had thought about it. Of course, she'd thought about it. Going after Mia, explaining all that had happened that night. What would that accomplish? The way Mia had talked about Cori today, things seemed painfully unresolved, and if Lauryn were to explain, what would stop Mia from reconciling with her ex? Engagements didn't end over drunken kisses, did they? If there was still something between Mia and Cori, they could make up. Lauryn's heart sunk at the thought. But maybe that was the least she could do. Maybe then Mia would be happy, and Lauryn could be okay with that outcome, right?

"Take it from someone who waited five years to confess their feelings. It'll hurt if she doesn't want you back..." Blake paused as if to make sure Lauryn was hearing her. "But it still hurts if you don't know."

"Yeah." Lauryn glanced at the darkening sky—winter days had always been so short. Her phone vibrated and she looked at it to see Blake's face had disappeared, replaced by an incoming call from Kelly, her publicist. She sent it to voicemail and Blake reemerged.

Blake glanced over at her shoulder, nodding to someone out of view. "I'll be right there." She turned to Lauryn again. "I've got to get back to the shoot. It might look like 100 degrees, but this breeze has a bite, and I can't have the model getting windchill."

Lauryn smiled. "Thanks, B."

"Always."

The call had barely disappeared when her phone started buzzing again.

Kelly.

Lauryn huffed, smashing her thumb against the answer button with unrestrained force. "I really can't talk right now, Kelz."

"Hello to you, too, Lauryn." She had that thing in her tone—a terseness reserved explicitly for times when Lauryn had created a mess she hadn't yet figured out how to clean up. "I thought when we agreed to let you stay in Denver without security it was because you needed to lay low."

Lauryn's brows met as she sat up in the loveseat. "I have been laying low. The only time I've even left this apartment is for business or to see Sully. No one's noticed me, Kelly."

"Then why did I get a tip that LA Now is planning on running an article on you titled *Has Lauryn Matthews traded her party days for a secret family?*"

The pace of Lauryn's heart picked up. "Excuse me?"

"They have a picture, Lo. The woman, the kids. It's beautiful, really, and not exactly negative press, but these are the kinds of things I need to know about before anyone else."

"What picture?"

"Outside a school? The angle isn't great. I don't think it was taken by paps. Probably a nosy parent."

Lauryn stood and started inside. "Do you have it? The picture."

"Yes, but I need you to talk to me, Lauryn. Who is she?"

"Send it to me. The article, too."

"Lauryn—"

"Please, Kelly. I'll tell you whatever you need to know later. There's somewhere I need to be first."

"If you're going to see her, I don't recommend it. For all we know, she staged this whole thing."

Lauryn grabbed the keys to her rental and the scarf she'd left on the sofa earlier. "Staged? For what purpose?"

"Don't be naïve, Lauryn."

"Send me the article. And try to stop them from running it. Offer an exclusive, whatever they want." Lauryn disconnected the call and left the apartment. She knew what Kelly was suggesting—it was her job to be skeptical of everything, everyone who got close to Lauryn, but there was no question in Lauryn's mind Mia had nothing to do with this. Her only concern was that Mia knew before the article came out. She didn't know how recognizable Mia, Bella and Zac were in that picture. This was someone's family, and not Lauryn's like LA Now was set to insinuate. And she didn't know how Mia would feel about having her niece and nephew plastered on the internet. She didn't know how Matthieu and Layla would feel.

Five minutes ago, on her call with Blake, Lauryn wasn't sure when she'd get the nerve to talk to Mia again, but here she was hopping into her car and hoping when she called, Mia answered the phone.

Mia hadn't picked up.

Not the first, second or fourth time Lauryn had called. When she finally decided to try the office instead, Arty had been kind enough to confirm with Darby and James that Mia wasn't with either of them, but had actually gone home after her last client, which was exactly how Lauryn had wound up outside Mia's door completely unannounced.

The tightness in her chest hadn't let up and she was

pretty sure Mia was exactly the kind of person who would not like someone just showing up. Did Lauryn really even need to be here, or had she convinced herself this was important enough because she desperately wanted to see Mia again, even with how they'd left things earlier? Especially with how they'd left things earlier. Maybe she should've just sent a text and waited for Mia to respond. Give her the option to call or ask to see Lauryn if she wanted to. That seemed better. Respecting her space.

She dipped into her back pocket for her phone and started tapping out a message.

The door swung open and her head snapped up.

"Lauryn?" Mia stood before her, hair caught in a messy bun, face makeup free, dressed in a cropped sweatshirt and lounge pants. And somehow, even with her heart rate doubled at having been caught out there like a total creeper, she wanted to smile. She'd seen Mia perfectly made up every kind of beautiful… except for this. And this was probably her favorite.

Not probably.

Absolutely.

"What are you doing here?"

Lauryn blinked. "Sorry. Your doorman. Apparently he saw us leave with Bella and Zac the other day, so he just let me up."

"Yeah. They called me. But that doesn't really answer my question."

If not for the softness of her tone, Lauryn may have taken that the wrong way. "I know. I—I just…Need to talk to you about something. It's kind of important."

Mia frowned, but stepped aside to let Lauryn in. It was only when Mia had shut the door and faced her again, had she noticed the phone in Mia's hand.

"Sorry. Were you in the middle of something? I could wait or leave. I tried to call before but..."

"Yeah." Mia pursed her lips. "Was on another call."

Lauryn stared at her, wanting to go closer, dare to touch her face like in the basement earlier. For a minute, Mia had seemed okay with that. She'd leaned into it, or was that wishful thinking?

"Lauryn, listen, if this is about earlier—"

Lauryn shook her head quickly. "It's not. Although, it could be. If you want. If you want to talk about it, I mean."

She could've imagined it, but a smile ghosted Mia's lips before she leaned against the door and asked, "What's up, Laur?"

Lauryn's eyes trailed her head to toe. Her position in combination with the way she'd taken to shortening Lauryn's name wasn't doing much for Lauryn's focus, or the rattle of her heart. As much as today had dwindled her hopes of them ever being anything more than realtor and client, that single endearment was enough to keep her helplessly deluded. "LA Now has a picture of us with Bella and Zac. They didn't get their faces, but they got yours. And from all indications, they're going to run an article on it."

Mia stood upright, placing her phone on a nearby end table before stepping closer. "An article saying what?"

It was barely a paragraph, more of a scoop than an article. Short enough for Lauryn to have read it on the elevator ride to Mia's floor. "Not much of anything. I've traded partying for family life in a Denver suburb." Lauryn scoffed. "It's kind of ridiculous, actually. The good thing is they don't seem to know who you are. The bad thing is, they'll most likely find out. And once that happens, they could show up at your job. They could show up here."

"They couldn't get into either."

"But you have to leave these places, Mia. You have to come and go."

"I can handle some idiot trying to take pictures of me."

"You don't know how relentless they can be." She turned, starting a slow pace along the foyer. "I mean, I told my publicist to stop it if she can, offer them something more interesting but there are never really any guarantees with these people, and after everything that's happened, especially now that I know about you and Cori, the last thing I wanted was to cause you anymore trouble—"

"Lauryn—"

"I didn't know, Mia. I would never have hurt you like that."

"You didn't even know me."

"But I do now." She stopped, chest heaving, eyes locked with Mia's. "I do now, Mia. So, tell me how to fix this and it's done. I can leave. What I said earlier stands. You don't ever have to see me again. Denver isn't exactly smal—" Lauryn stumbled as Mia's lips met hers, firm and soft and more intense than she'd ever imagined. Her hands found Mia's hips, pulling her closer and her grip tightened at the touch of Mia's bare skin.

She hummed, biting down on Lauryn's lips and Lauryn felt it in the depths of her stomach, lower.

"Wait, wait, wait." She pulled away, trying and failing to catch her breath. "This doesn't seem like a good idea."

"It probably isn't." Mia adjusted her arms around Lauryn's neck. "But I really want to keep kissing you right now. Is that okay?"

"Are you sure?" Lauryn angled her head to close the height gap between them, brushing their lips together.

"Yes." Mia undid Lauryn's scarf then took her hand, leading her toward the all-white sofa in the living room. Her free hand went to Lauryn's chest—her eyes the darkest brown Lauryn had ever seen, even in the poorly lit entryway at Revel on New Year's Eve—and she pushed until Lauryn was seated.

Lauryn took a slow gulp, reverent in her attentiveness, as Mia straddled her and repositioned her hands around Lauryn's neck. "Mia."

"Shh."

This kiss was softer, more meaningful. Purposeful? And Lauryn let herself get lost in it—the silk and fire of Mia's lips, taste of her tongue, weight of her body and thread of her fingers through Lauryn's hair. The turtleneck that had kept Lauryn warm for most of the day felt suffocating, a barrier she desperately wanted out of their way. She tried not to overcompensate by moving her hands too high beneath Mia's crop top. It was enough this way. She would live in this bubble of Mia's subtle but intense perfume, kissing her like this all night if she could.

Mia's hips shifted slightly, and Lauryn tried to ignore the throbbing between her thighs. Hands went to the hem of her sweater, and though Mia's mouth never left hers, she managed to make out, "Can I take this off?"

Lauryn's hands were up before she even thought about it, the turtleneck tugged over her head and tossed somewhere out of view. Mia's lips went to her neck, her collarbone, curve of her shoulder. "Mia."

She met her gaze, lips red and parted. "Too fast?"

"No." Lauryn cradled her face. "Not at all. I just—" Of all the reactions she'd been expecting on her way over, this never entered her imagination. She wanted so badly to make sense of what was happening, why it was happening. More than that, she needed to know there was even the slightest possibility it could happen again. She didn't know that she could handle having Mia like this only to never have her again. She stroked her cheek. "You have no idea how much I want this."

"I think I do." Mia licked her lips, and Lauryn couldn't help tracing her thumb over them. "I did feel it, too. In your car that night. I feel it now. And I don't know how to explain it, Laur. I don't know what kind of karmic trick the universe is trying to play on us, but after earlier at the house, what you said about never seeing you again, I didn't know what I wanted, but I knew that wasn't it."

Lauryn's fingers continued their dance down Mia's neck.

"That is really distracting."

"Is it?" She held Mia's gaze, searching as she trailed the side of her breast, pausing when she realized there were no ridges beneath the sweatshirt. No bra. She brushed a tentative thumb over her nipple.

Mia's eyes fell shut. "Very distracting."

Lauryn kissed her neck, then pulled back to take her shirt off too. She placed both hands just beneath the underside of Mia's breasts, resuming her kisses when she asked, "How far are we planning to take this?"

"As far as we want."

"Yeah?"

"Yes." She ground down on Lauryn's hips again, and reached to unclasp her bra.

Lauryn pulled her closer, both moaning at the brush of their nipples, the feeling of their bodies pressed together, their kiss faster, deeper.

"Lauryn."

Lauryn clenched her thighs tighter, hands itching to move lower, to slip between them and into the waistband of Mia's pants. Mia leaned back enough to take both Lauryn's breasts in her hands, tease and twist her nipples. Clearly, she didn't plan on going easy on her, but Lauryn loved that. She loved the buildup as much as the crash, and she loved a woman who knew exactly what she wanted. She broke the kiss, finally caving, being bold enough to slide her fingers into Mia's underwear and down to her clit to find her wet and yielding.

The way Mia's grip tightened made her wish she'd done it about five minutes ago.

She glided her fingers through Mia's arousal to her core and back up to her clit, whispering, "Is this how you like it?"

"Inside. Now."

Lauryn breathed a laugh, sliding her fingers into place, but just outside where Mia wanted them. "Are you asking or telling?"

"Telling." She held Lauryn's hand steady, moaning as they slipped in.

"Fuck, Mia." Lauryn drove her fingers deeper, bringing her free hand to Mia's chin. She needed to look her in the eyes for this, needed an imprint of the sheer pleasure on Mia's face seared into her mind forever, the image of her knit brows and bottom lip trapped between her teeth and the way she mumbled things like yes, god, Laur, please, harder.

Lauryn ignored the burn in her wrist, rubbing tight circles against Mia's clit with her thumb, fulfilling Mia's every command and when she could feel the tremor in her legs, Lauryn knew she was right on the edge.

"Lauryn." She pressed their foreheads together. "Laur— Oh my God—Fuck."

Lauryn let her ride it out, lips and fingers soft all the way through, and she couldn't take her eyes off her if she tried. Gradually, Mia's grip loosened, her breathing slowing by the second, and Lauryn's pulse racing to a crash. She brushed a thumb over Mia's cheek, gazing at her like she'd just witnessed something otherworldly. "Damn."

"I know." Mia threaded her fingers through Lauryn's hair again, both still catching their breaths, Lauryn tracing shapes along Mia's sides. Mia pressed a slow kiss to her lips and then she shuffled off Lauryn's lap to slip out of her lounge pants, leaving only a simple black thong in its place.

Lauryn blinked in complete awe of her—the glow of her skin, curve of her hips and thighs—as she stepped forward and brought her hands to the button of Lauryn's jeans.

"Take these off."

Lauryn nodded her compliance and Mia kneeled between her legs, starting with her shoes before taking off her jeans and underwear, and leaving them on the floor. She tugged Lauryn to the edge of the couch with surprising force and pressed a kiss to her navel, humming as she rubbed Lauryn's clit with two fingers. "God, you're so wet."

Lauryn dragged in a breath. She didn't want this to be over. She wasn't ready for it to be over, but after watching Mia come like that, she knew there was little she could do to ward off her own climax if Mia kept touching her. "Mia, I can't—I'm going to—"

"I know." Mia nodded, lips brushing Lauryn's thigh. She trailed her free hand from Lauryn's ankle along her calf to the back of her knee, pushing Lauryn's leg onto her shoulder, lips hovering right where Lauryn needed them. "Just look me in the eyes when you do."

CHAPTER 13

Mia's heart hadn't stopped racing. Not since the moment she'd pressed her lips to Lauryn's an hour ago. Two? She'd willingly lost track of time, given in to the brush of Lauryn's fingers, the taste of her tongue, her skin, the way her body tightened all over when she came, eyes amber and fire and just... Mia's heart hadn't stopped racing even now that they'd been lying in her bed staring at each other for the longest time. And that was exactly how she knew she was in trouble. So much fucking trouble.

Her eyes trailed the motion as Lauryn's fingers danced along the tips of hers, the contact faint yet electrifying. She knew better than to make too much of the feeling in her chest. There were so many ways to rationalize it, but every time their eyes met all those reasons evaporated. "What are you thinking?"

Lauryn walked her middle and ring finger into Mia's palm, eyes glued to the movement. "That I'm afraid to ruin this moment with words."

A second passed. Mia nodded. "I get that." She wrapped her hand around Lauryn's and tugged lightly. "Come here."

From her current position, halfway down Mia's king bed, lying on her stomach with her legs bent at the knees in a gentle sway, the arch of her back and curve of her ass on full display, Lauryn was just the right amount of consuming to make sure Mia would never forget this image of her. Mia needed her closer still.

Lauryn shuffled up the bed and folded one arm beneath her head. There was a demure to her that Mia hadn't exactly noticed before, but now that she had didn't seem out of character even for someone who performed in front of thousands, who was known to half the country for partying, drugs, women. All of which seemed so unlike the Lauryn she'd come to know over the last two weeks. Had it only been two weeks?

Lauryn started a masterpiece of indistinguishable shapes on Mia's thigh and Mia ignored the clench in her stomach to push a few locks of hair out of Lauryn's face.

"Is it really everything you want? The house."

Lauryn hummed a laugh, closing her eyes as Mia's hand delved deeper into the lush curls of her hair. "That's what's on your mind?"

"Among other things." Mia slid down the headboard to lie next to her. "But yes, I do actually want to know, Laur."

"I love it when you call me that."

Mia had slipped when she'd first called her "Laur" earlier at the house. They may have been fighting. She may have been angry and hurt and somehow defending Cori in her bid to help Lauryn understand why this hasn't been easy for her, but nicknames were part of her love language —one of the things she'd always shared with Darby and James—and if her mouth had gone ahead of her brain and given Lauryn one, there was little she could do about it.

"It is everything I want," Lauryn finally said. "I think I've imagined a whole life there already. Is that weird?"

Mia smiled, shaking her head. "Not at all. It's usually part of how you know."

Lauryn moved her shapes higher, swirling around Mia's navel and Mia took her hand to stop the movement. They could do that, or they could talk, but Mia didn't have the capacity for both now that she knew exactly what it was like to have those fingers inside her. And right now, talking seemed important. Talking was her mind's way of processing things, usually after an eternity of pretending they didn't exist. "Did you mean what you said about us never seeing each other again?"

Lauryn opened her eyes. "If that's what you want, yes."

"What do you want, Laur?"

"Isn't it obvious?"

Mia shook her head. "I want to say, yes, but not really. You're not what I expected. I mean, you crashed into me looking like you just stumbled off a boat in Alaska and I haven't been able to shake you since. You're all I think about Lauryn. For different reasons at first, but..." Mia licked her lips. "You gift boxes of sunshine to people who probably don't deserve it and give third and fourth chances to people you're paying, and you're fucking incredible with kids you've never met...and you"—Mia's forehead creased—"throw drug-fueled Hollywood parties and are almost never seen with the same woman twice? I don't get it."

For a while, Lauryn stared at the sliver of space between them, thumb stroking the back of Mia's hand, and then she said, "It was a surprise party. A celebration if I won the Best New Artist nom, an 'oh well' if I didn't. The label planned it. All I did was show up. I don't do drugs, Mia. Never have.

And I've seen what it does to someone who's everything to me, so I don't think I ever will. As for the women...Well, I don't really think that's anyone's business."

Mia swallowed, processing the answer.

"But since it's you that's asking." Lauryn looked at her again. "Connections have always been hard for me. I've just never been any good at them. Not with any of my dozen foster parents or siblings, or handful of friends. I guess it's been like that with dating, too. Maybe it has something to do with my parents giving me up for whatever reason. Maybe I struggle with meaningful connection because the people who were meant to teach me were never there in the first place. I don't know. I'm sure my therapist has a few theories. But the connections I do feel..." Her hand tightened around Mia's. "I don't let go of them easily."

Mia's other hand settled on her face, and she wanted to say something. She just wasn't sure what.

"I'm sorry. About Cori. Nothing happened, besides the kiss I mean, and if you wanted to..." Her jaw clenched. "Make up with her, you should. If anything, I was her drunken mistake, and I don't know anything about marriage, but I don't know if that should end one. Potential marriage, I guess."

Mia sighed. It wasn't as if she had never thought about forgiving Cori. She'd thought about it even when she'd believed Cori and Lauryn had done a lot more than kiss. Because that's what people did when they loved someone, right? Forgave them. But the more she dwelled on it in the days after the Instagram story had been leaked, the more her anger had simmered to a sort of awareness that Cori kissing Lauryn may have been the catalyst to the end of her relationship with Mia, but there was so much more that had been wrong between them. At her worst, Cori was narcissistic and indifferent, and probably manipulative at her best. The things she'd told Mia, promised her—the marriage, the life of scheduling breakfast and trips and skip days once a year just to whisk their imagined kids off to a movie and gelato—were never things she actually wanted, too. They were things she'd told Mia to keep her. Maybe that's what Mia's parents and brother had seen. The reason they were civil at most. The reason James and Darby had always been cautiously supportive.

Somewhere beyond the confines of Mia's bedroom, a series of dings sounded then a phone started ringing. Lauryn glanced over her shoulder then back to Mia.

"Is that yours?" Mia asked.

"Probably."

"You should get it."

Lauryn shook her head. "It can wait."

It was the answer Mia had wanted, even subconsciously, but she was so attuned to answering her phone whenever it rang—always a client or James or Darby or her family calling—she would've understood if Lauryn needed to go check hers. The ringing stopped and she opened her mouth to pick up where they had left off when the noise started again, this time joined by hers. "Okay, is there a fire we should know about?"

Lauryn laughed. "I hope not." And then her brows drew closer. "Fuck. Please tell me they didn't." She shifted to the edge of the bed and stood.

Mia tried to ignore her retreating form in all its naked glory—the curve of hips and thighs, shape of her legs. "Didn't what, Laur?"

No answer.

She rolled her eyes, draping a tangle of sheets around her as she followed into the living room and picked up her phone as Lauryn tended to hers. Her heart clenched at the caller ID. Cori Norman.

"Mia?"

Mia blinked, looking up at Lauryn. "Sorry, what?"

"The article. They ran it."

Mia glanced down at her phone as the ringing continued. The last time they'd spoken was...four months ago. It had taken half as long for Cori to finally stop calling, stop texting, stop showing up to the apartment Mia had left the second her lease was up. Mia could've sworn she'd deleted Cori's number.

"Are you going to get that?" Lauryn came to stop in front of her, and Mia knew she'd seen the name on the screen. "Oh." She took a step back. "You should probably get that."

The ringing stopped. Mia mumbled, "No."

Lauryn's gaze shifted to the floor and she crossed the room as if in search of something.

This time, a single chime drew Mia's attention. A text. *Please pick up. I just want to talk.*

"I'm going to go."

"Wait, what?" Mia shook her head, looking up to find Lauryn already dressed in the turtleneck she'd been wearing earlier. "Lauryn."

"My publicist keeps calling and I have a million mentions online." She buttoned her jeans. "I need to take care of this."

"Okay, but we shoul—"

"It's okay, Mia." Her lips stretched in a wistful smile, her eyes bright beneath the beam of the overhead lamp. "Some things aren't meant to be more than they are."

"Lauryn..."

"Answer your phone, Mia."

Mia tuned in to the ringing of her phone again. The next thing she heard was the clank of her front door.

THIS WAS one of the things about Cori Mia had never been in love with. She loved an argument. More than that, she loved to win an argument, usually by guilting the other person into believing they'd wronged her somehow. Mia breathed a heavy sigh, pressing fingers to her eyes. Half an hour ago when Lauryn had left, she'd told herself that letting her go was the right thing to do. At least for now. There would come a time when they'd have to finish their conversation, talk about the amazing night they'd been having together and what it meant, but Cori hadn't stopped calling and maybe there was a part of Mia that felt like the sooner she handled things with Cori, the sooner she could finally put it all behind her.

"You realize how much of a hypocrite this makes you?" Cori chastised.

"This isn't the same, and don't try to pretend it is. You went away for a weekend and couldn't keep your tongue in your own mouth."

"And this thing with you and Lauryn is supposed to be what, Mia? Revenge?"

"Oh my God." Mia dropped her head back against the sofa, gazing up at the ceiling. "Do you even fucking hear yourself? Do you think I wanted this? I was going to marry you, Cori! You ruined it. You broke us. Not me. Actually..." She paused, taking a breath. "I think we both know we were already broken."

"That's not true."

"Who stopped it?"

"Stopped what?"

"The kiss," Mia clarified. "Who stopped it from going further?"

"I did! Of course I stopped it as soon as I realized what was happening."

Mia hummed, nodding at the inflection in Cori's tone, the way whenever she was lying, she always felt the need to double down, try to make her answer that much more convincing. How ironic. "You never were a good liar."

"Mia..."

"It's over, Cori. Not because of Lauryn. Not because you kissed her. Not because I did. It was never going to work. We never wanted the same things, and you pretending we did is probably exactly how you wound up at that party, drunk in another woman's lap in the first place. Please stop making this harder than it has to be."

Cori's end of the line remained quiet, only the faint sound of her breathing to give away her presence, and Mia knew her declaration had hit. "So, it's true then," Cori muttered softly. "You two are dating."

"We're not dating."

"Then what, Mia?" Cori yelled, her tone octaves higher again, set for round two. "Are you introducing all your clients to your brother's kids now?"

Mia sighed. "I don't know, Cori. But I do know what Lauryn and I are to each other is none of your business. Not anymore. Please stop calling me." She ended the call on Cori's response and tossed the phone on the sofa next to her. There was every chance Cori would call again—she was relentless that way—but Mia meant what she'd said. She'd meant it four, six months ago, and nothing Cori said would change her mind. Now more than ever, she was certain of it.

Her gaze drifted to the black cable knit scarf draped over the arm of the chair and she reached for it, testing the fabric between her fingers. In her rush to leave earlier, Lauryn must have forgotten it. The smell of her lingered in the air—vanilla, roses, and something more organic at its core, something distinctly Lauryn. Mia thought back to the two of them earlier, in nearly the same spot she sat in now. Lauryn's hands on her, tentative yet sure, the way she constantly sought Mia's consent to go further with every step. And it was hot and impulsive and sexy, but it reaffirmed everything she'd been gradually realizing about Lauryn since the day they'd met, that had kept her up two nights ago after they'd dropped off Bella and Zac. Lauryn was nothing like Mia had thought, and Mia couldn't rewrite their history, but there was no point denying she wanted more. More unexpected talks where Lauryn revealed a bit more of herself every time. More chances for Mia to stay, listen, and hopefully, more of the moments they'd shared tonight before LA Now and Cori had swept in to ruin it.

Mia picked up her phone, trying not to overthink it when she swiped her way to Lauryn's contact and tapped out a text: I know you're probably busy right now, but I'd really like to finish our talk. *Would breakfast on Sunday be okay?*

Was a day enough for Lauryn to get things settled? Maybe Mia should've waited for her to call or text if she wanted to. But with the way she had left, the look on her face when she'd seen Cori's name on Mia's phone, Mia needed Lauryn to know that there was nothing left between her and Cori. Not that she was ready to hop into another relationship now, either. Was she ready for another relationship? That's something she should probably have figured out before she talked to Lauryn again.

But maybe she didn't need to after all.

Because Lauryn didn't answer Mia's text, and she didn't call.

Not that night.

The next day, or a week later.

CHAPTER 14

Lauryn twisted the knob of the blue door to Sully's office after her fourth unanswered knock. Locked. She pursed her lips, head slightly tilted as she reached into her pocket for her phone. Sully hadn't answered her text, but it was nice to know that LA Now was still keeping tabs on her.

Singer, songwriter Lauryn Matthews spotted leaving DEN. Back to visit the family?

She huffed—*where do they even get this shit?*—rolling her eyes as she stuffed the phone back into her pocket and started down the short hallway to Revel's main floor. A remixed Janelle Monáe boomed from the speakers, the lounge rowdy with its Super Bowl watch party. She lowered her head and moved toward the bar, determined to not let her mind drift to the headline she'd just seen. Determined not to think of the implication that Mia was her family or wonder what she'd been up to the last week. Had she spent every waking moment reliving that night, too? Did memories of Lauryn's taste and smell and moans haunt her the way hers did Lauryn? Did she still think about after? The intensity of being in each other's presence, the vulnerability in the silence, the talking.

Probably not.

Maybe she'd made up with Cori that night and invited Lauryn to breakfast Sunday only to salvage their professional relationship. Maybe she hadn't. Either way, Lauryn hadn't answered the text, and if paparazzi and her ex or Lauryn's involvement in the end of her engagement hadn't ruined it, Lauryn's self-sabotage had definitely done the job. Isn't that why Mia had had Arty send over the contracts for the house instead of doing it herself? No call, no email. Nothing.

Lauryn stopped by the bar and waved to get the attention of one of the bartenders, Hannah. Surely, she'd know why Sully was MIA.

"Lo?"

Lauryn barely caught her name over the blare of the music. The last thing she wanted was to be recognized here, but the use of her nickname echoed familiarity and she turned without reservation to find Astrid next to her. "Hey, Ash." She narrowed her gaze, taking in Astrid's leather jacket and slicked back hair—a few unruly strands falling into her face as usual. Not her typical get-up for working the entrance. "Not working tonight?"

"No." Astrid's grin carried a secret, like words unsaid, but all she gave away was, "I'm actually headed to a party. You looking for Sul?"

"Yeah. I checked her office but no luck."

"She took the night off for a date with the wife. No phones thing."

"Shit. That's tonight?"

Astrid nodded. "Yup."

Lauryn worried her bottom lip. Going back to the apartment alone was a terrible idea. She was too wired to write, sleep or even do anything as mindless as watching TV.

"You want to come to this party? I know you only hang out here when Sully's around." Astrid rubbed the back of her neck. "And if I'm being honest, you'd kind of be doing me a solid."

Lauryn's brows drew together. "What do you mean?"

"So, there's this girl—"

"Of course." Lauryn laughed.

Astrid chuckled. "I know, I know, but both her best friends are going to be there. And I'm not talking call-up-and-chat-every-once-in-a-while friends. I mean she's really sweet and I really like her but I know if I screw it up my-mom-would-probably-never-see-my-body kind of friends."

Lauryn's eyes widened in amusement. "Intense." But who didn't want to share that kind of connection with someone? She sighed, considering it. "What kind of party is this? Because I can't—"

"Super Bowl. Very lowkey. At her house. You'll get recognized by one person, if it at all."

"And she's good with you inviting a stranger to her place?"

Astrid dug her phone out of her jacket pocket. "Why don't we find out?"

THE LAST THING Lauryn wanted to do was go to a party after the week she'd had. A week in LA, hounded by her manager Ken and publicist Kelly and three too-many meetings with the label, had done everything to reassert her decision to buy a house in Denver. Not to mention the pair of paparazzi who had cameras in her face the moment she'd exited LAX a week ago. Kelly, for her part, had the foresight to send Ellis—Lauryn's well-over six feet tall, and weirdly chatty bodyguard—to the airport ahead of time. Lauryn was grateful, truly, but she also happened to be convinced Ellis attracted more attention than not, which was exactly how she'd gotten them to agree to let her return to Denver alone. Then again, based on her last meeting with Ken, the label was prepared to ride the convenience of this surge in her mentions by releasing the only single she'd recorded so far.

Tonight.

She figured there was little harm in accompanying Astrid, though. Hardly anyone in Denver seemed to care who she was and maybe a night spent with a few perfectly normal football fans would stop her mind from drifting to Mia every two seconds. The only problem was, Lauryn knew next to nothing about football and Astrid's twenty-minute lesson on the Lyft ride over had only equipped her with enough knowledge to be further confused.

The car rolled to a stop in front of a quaint two-story and Astrid reached across the backseat to squeeze Lauryn's shoulder. "Just cheer when they cheer." She pushed the door open and exited the car.

Lauryn blinked, following. "Right. Sounds like a plan."

They crossed a stone walkway toward a baroque wine-colored door with a small wreath still hung and Astrid rang the doorbell. So, this woman Astrid liked was one of those people who kept her decorations up for weeks after Christmas. Astrid turned to Lauryn. "I should probably warn you...she's a bit on the bright side. Darby. James, one the best friends, kind of goes against the grain, and Mia—"

The door swung open to reveal a beaming Arty, dressed in a Broncos shirt and Chino shorts. "Ms. Sucre!"

Lauryn winced at Arty's use of her last name, her head

spinning from Astrid's earlier explanation. "This is Jane Darby's house?"

"Yes?" Astrid frowned. "You two know each other?"

Arty waved them in. "Come in, come in. The game's about to start."

Lauryn entered the house tentatively, heart racing, eyes instantly scanning for Mia. She'd only spent a little over an hour with Mia, Darby and James under the same roof, but suddenly Astrid's analogy made sense—the kind of friends who'd help hide a body. It was just in the way they related. Her mind flashed back to a week ago. Darby's polite probing, James' watchful stare, at least before she'd disappeared upstairs. They were protective of Mia, and now that Lauryn understood why, she couldn't blame them. She even respected them for it, but if she had known this was Darby's house, she would never have shown up here.

"Ash..."

Astrid started through the living room and Lauryn followed, glancing behind and around her. The room hummed with quiet chatter and a Carly Rae Jepsen song played softly in the background. A pair of commentators exchanged muted arguments on a large flat screen set in the entertainment stand against one wall. Strange, for a watch party, but the six or so people in the room all seemed occupied with talking to each other. An anxious gulp slid down her throat at the thought of Mia emerging any second.

"Hey, you made it!"

Lauryn almost crashed into Astrid's back at the sound of Darby's voice, but she looked up just in time to catch herself. She straightened, aiming for casual, but the smile she offered Darby was likely ten kinds of awkward.

Darby grinned, glancing from her to Astrid. "How did I not know that you know Lauryn?"

"I feel like I should be surprised that *you* know Lauryn," said Astrid. "But, honestly, last night you almost made friends with a pigeon."

"Pigeons are really misunderstood. They're actually very smart."

Lauryn watched the exchange with creased brows. She was pretty sure this was flirting, but she and Mia never talked about pigeons. Why was Darby being so nice, anyway? Had Mia not mentioned what had happened between them? Then again, she could hardly imagine Darby not being polite under any circumstance. She leaned in, placing a kiss on Darby's cheek. "Thanks for having me, Darby."

"Lauryn?"

Lauryn looked up and found Mia's gaze on her. Not that she needed to. No one said her name the way Mia did. She parted her lips to release a slow breath, her pulse racing, her entire body on edge with their sudden proximity. An inch away, Astrid and Darby carried on a conversation about silly hats and personalized jerseys, probably like the one Mia was wearing. The one that didn't seem purposely paired with her form-fitting ankle pants and Louboutins. Not a football fan either, then. A smile tugged at Lauryn's lips as she met Mia's gaze again—makeup and hair flawless as always—and then her mind conjured her last memory of Mia. Hair in a messy bun, dressed in a cropped sweatshirt and lounge pants, hands and lips like fire on Lauryn's skin.

Mia stepped closer, her perfume subtle but intoxicating. "What are you doing here?"

"I uh—I didn't know it was Darby's party. I was just at the club and—" She cut herself off. "I'll just go."

Mia studied her for a moment before dropping her gaze. "I texted you."

"I know."

"So why didn't you text back?"

Lauryn's lips parted and closed. "I had to go back to LA for a couple of days, and I guess I just thought maybe it was better if I gave you some space."

"Better for who, Laur?"

"You..." Lauryn stared at her—her teakwood eyes gleaming despite her obvious confusion. The rest of the sentence lingered like poison on Lauryn's tongue. "And Cori."

Mia narrowed her eyes at her. "Lauryn—" She cut herself off with a shake of her head then took Lauryn's hand and started out of the room, back into the foyer and up the stairs.

Something about being led this way sent Lauryn seven years into the past to her days at UCLA and being more than willing to help Drew's this-doesn't-mean-I'm-gay sorority sister explore her curiosities. Getting her naked was probably the furthest thing from Mia's mind right now, but it was better that way. For so many reasons.

Mia opened the first of three doors in a short hallway on the second floor and gestured for Lauryn to enter first. A light flipped on, bathing chiffon walls in the soft glow and revealing a well-made queen-sized bed, work desk and simple chest of drawers. For a bedroom, it seemed strangely unoccupied, definitely not very Darby.

"It's a guest room," Mia said almost as if reading Lauryn's mind. "She keeps it like this for whenever her parents visit. Peter and Debs are kind of...dull."

Lauryn nodded, facing Mia. The moment dragged, her eyes roaming over Mia's soft, umber skin, the dark liner around her eyes, neutral lipstick on her perfectly plump lips. Her hair had been pushed back behind both ears, exposing the subtle cut of her jaw, and flowed in straight locks down her back. Once again, the Broncos jersey she wore seemed out of place, but the name Stone printed on the back gave a clear indication it had been made for her.

"Lauryn."

Lauryn wanted to default to something easy—joke about Mia being a forced team player, or ask how her day had been, if she'd come to Darby's straight from the office—but they might as well get this over with. "I'm sorry I didn't answer. I wanted to. Trust me, I wanted to, especially after —" She sighed. "I wanted to, Mia."

Mia stepped closer, bringing a hand to Lauryn's chin, making sure they were looking at each other. "Cori and I are done. We were done long before you and I collided on New Year's Eve, before you walked into my office that Monday, and what you saw last week... Her calling, my hesitation. It has nothing to do with me wanting her back or trying to fix things between us. I guess it just caught me off guard." She brushed a hand against Lauryn's cheek then wrapped both around her neck, her heels leaving them at almost equal height. "And if it wasn't for everything that happened with that article and your publicist calling and all that, I would've never let you out my door without talking about what this means."

Lauryn brought a tentative hand to Mia's hips. "What do you want it to mean?"

Mia smiled, glancing skyward for a moment. "I don't know. More than that you were the person my ex kissed before she was my ex? It still feels crazy, but it's hard to even think about you that way anymore. It's like I created this version of you that was so easy to hate, because that's the only way I could process what happened, but then you walked into my office and you flipped everything I thought I knew on its head."

Lauryn was sure Mia could hear her heart hammering inside her chest. She closed the gap between them, wrapping her arms around Mia's waist, holding her closer. If she could keep her there, if she could feel the warmth and silk of her skin, bask in the rush of her perfume, then it was real.

"You are so beautiful, Laur. Body and soul. And I don't know what it means that I'd sworn off romance, relationships, all of it until you, but I know I don't care. All I want is to get to know you. If you'll let me."

Lauryn stared down at her, shaking her head. All the words her mind conjured felt scattered and inadequate. She thought about the last week, about how she'd gone back to LA determined to shield Mia from all the Hollywood trash that found Lauryn sometimes, about the exclusive she'd promised LA Now in exchange for not publishing Mia's name, about how she would have done it all even if Mia had gone back to Cori. And she thought about how Blake had described falling for Drew as a constant rollercoaster of dread and euphoria. And maybe it was too soon to know, but Lauryn had never been as scared to lose someone as she'd been when she saw Cori's name on Mia's phone last week, and she'd never been happier than she was now. *So, this is what it feels like.*

Mia smiled as Lauryn brushed their lips together. "Well, aren't you going to say something?"

Lauryn nodded, breathing, "Yes."

"Yes, what, Laur?" Mia laughed.

"Yes, Mia." Lauryn cradled her cheeks, kissing her gently. "Yes, to all of it. And so much more."

CHAPTER 15

Mia's head snapped up at the knock on her door and the pounding in her chest picked up. She released a slow breath, clenching and unclenching her hands as she gave herself a final once over in the mirror. The elegant black dress she'd settled on melded to her body in all the right places, but the long cardigan she'd paired it with was perfect for a cozy night in. Even if it was Valentine's Day. Another series of raps echoed on the door and she started toward it in a light jog, bare feet tapping against the hardwood floors.

She paused at the door, hand on the knob and she dragged in a breath before swinging it open.

Lauryn stood in the doorway—eyes alight with the glow of her smile, hair in perfect curls down to her shoulders, wearing an open wrap jacket and matching pants. Mia's gaze trailed down to the pair of pointed toe boots on Lauryn's feet then back up the sliver of her abdomen and glimpse of her bra left on display. Mia's lips parted then closed. "Hi?"

Lauryn laughed, stepping closer as she pressed a kiss to Mia's lips. "Hi, yourself." She brushed her nose against Mia's cheek, the height difference between them exaggerated with the rare instance of Lauryn wearing heels and Mia not. "You smell incredible."

"You *look* incredible." Mia's hands drifted to Lauryn's waist, tracing her bare skin beneath the open flaps of her jacket. "God, how are you not freezing in this?"

"The way you're touching me right now is pretty helpful." She brought her lips to Mia's again, kissing her slowly, pulling her closer. "But if we keep this up, we are never making it to dinner, and you promised me the best roasted salmon I'll ever have, courtesy of Casa de Mia."

"Oh, did I?"

"Mhm. I believe you said it would be…" She trailed off, bringing her lips to Mia's ear. "Orgasmic."

Mia tossed her head back in a laugh, both hands on Lauryn's face—always needing to touch her whenever they were close, especially after three days of being apart. "I missed you."

"I missed you too, baby."

She closed her eyes, and for a moment, they just hugged. It was all so surreal. She still wasn't used to being with Lauryn this way. The traces of roses and vanilla on her skin; the security of her hugs and warmth of her endearments. The way she always seemed to know exactly what Mia needed, but was never afraid to ask whenever she didn't. Inside and out of the bedroom, the sofa, the backseat of her car, Mia's desk at the office… The way she trusted Mia enough to share things she kept from the rest of the world—music the label wouldn't let her record, Sully, her heart. It had only been six weeks since they'd met, but Mia couldn't help feeling like maybe it was time they called it what it was. But was Lauryn ready for that? Was Mia ready to trust someone so completely again?

Lauryn pulled away slowly, her brows raised. "You okay?"

"I'm great." Mia smiled, bobbing her head toward the bottle she only just noticed Lauryn had been holding. "What do you have there?"

"Krug Clos du Mesnil," Lauryn pronounced with exaggerated enunciation. She breathed a laugh. "Gift from Blake and Drew. For us."

Mia's heart clenched as she accepted the bottle. "I'll have to send them a thank you." She started toward the kitchen in search of her decanter, her mind stuck on the 'for us' Lauryn had tacked on to the end of her statement. "You told your friends about us?"

"Yeah."

The door shut and Mia anticipated the tap of Lauryn's heels following her into the kitchen as she focused on pouring the wine. The music playing from her living room faded, replaced by another Khalid song. Hands slowly slid around her waist, and she tensed for a second before relaxing.

"You told Darby and James, didn't you?"

"I tell Darby and James everything."

"Mia…"

Mia turned at her gentle probing and when their eyes met, and their toes grazed, she realized why she hadn't heard Lauryn approach.

"Is that why you wanted to stay in tonight?" Lauryn's gaze fell. "Do you not want people to know about this?"

"Laur, hey." Mia shook her head, resting a hand on Lauryn's chin. She could have laughed at the absurdity of it, but that probably wouldn't help. "That is not why I asked if you wanted to come here. Darbs and James were still putting finishing touches on the house, and I figured you probably wouldn't want to be anywhere we might get photographed. But I would've gone anywhere with you tonight. *Anywhere.* It's just...Blake and Drew are your people, your family. Telling them kind of seems like a big deal."

"This is a big deal. Isn't it?"

"It is."

"Mia..." She closed her eyes, her hands rubbing back and forth around Mia's waist, their lips touching as the tension built. "I—I think I'm—"

"Don't say it." Mia trailed her fingers down Lauryn's face to wrap both arms around her neck. "Not tonight. Tell me tomorrow, or the day after that. Tell me next week." A part of her wanted, more than anything, to hear the words Lauryn had been trying to get out. But there was something frail about grand declarations on Valentine's Day. Not that her heart didn't beat with all the yearning and love of forever right then. She whispered her next words onto Lauryn's lips, threading her fingers into her hair. "We deserve to take our time with this, Laur. I want to take my time with you. Is that okay?"

"I want that, too." Lauryn turned, leading Mia backward until she was pinned against the island, before sliding her onto the countertop.

They would never make it to dinner.

"You're wearing your thoughts on your face." Lauryn smiled, stepping between Mia's thighs. "But this incredibly intimate position is only so you have to look at me when I say I want you, Mia. I *only* want you. And I don't need a label. But I do need you to know that. Whether we only tell our friends, or we tell the world, I'm yours."

Mia took Lauryn's face in her hands as she leaned in. The second their lips touched, she knew they'd be having cold salmon for dinner. She wrapped her legs around Lauryn and Lauryn pulled her to the edge of the counter, deepening the kiss with a brush of her tongue. Her hands moved to Mia's legs, lingering at the hem of her dress and a coil tightened between her thighs. Mia loved her power suits as much as she craved control in the bedroom, but three days apart, with words like *I'm yours* hanging between them, and everything in her wanted to beg for it. "*Laur.*"

Lauryn nodded, shifting her grip. "Bed."

Mia shook her head. "Right here. Please."

"Right here?" Lauryn's brows inched up and, for a second, her gaze shifted as if scouting the kitchen for a better alternative.

"No?"

"No. I mean, yes." Her chest heaved as she shrugged off her jacket, revealing her breasts hugged in a black lace bra. She closed the gap between them again and her lips grazed Mia's ear, sending a shiver down her spine. "Just making sure we're not about to make a mess of dinner."

Mia clutched her tighter. "I will make you dinner for the rest of our lives if you stop talking and touch me."

"I am touching you, baby." She pushed off Mia's cardigan and nipped at her shoulder, her other hand in teasing strokes against Mia's inner thighs.

There was a very fundamental instinct in Mia that appealed to terms of endearment, especially when she was this turned on, especially whispered with that husk in Lauryn's voice. She tilted her head back as Lauryn trailed kisses down the column of her neck, her chest and breasts, between her ribs, burning a trail straight to her navel. The dress clinging to her body was way too warm, but she wasn't about to stop Lauryn's current path.

Lauryn slid the hem of her dress higher. "There are so many things I want to do to you."

Mia gripped the edge of the counter. "Want to start with just one?" Fingers slipped beneath the underside of her thong, dragging a moan from the back of her throat and maybe, just maybe, she was starting to rethink asking Lauryn to fuck her on this countertop. The quartz was cold and jagged in her palms and she was probably, definitely, about to make a mess of it. *"Lauryn."*

"I need this off."

She lifted her ass and Lauryn tugged off her underwear, leaving it around one ankle and all Mia could do was whimper and weave one hand into Lauryn's hair when Lauryn's tongue finally found her clit. Mia tensed, her body taut with the buildup, with the delicate strokes of Lauryn's tongue and thrust of her fingers. She let herself float away in the feeling of having Lauryn, of being had by Lauryn, and she tried not to think about what Lauryn said earlier. About only wanting Mia, about being Mia's. It felt like forever since she'd wanted anyone the way she wanted Laur, since she wanted to be anyone's person. But she did. She wanted to be Lauryn's in every possible way.

Lauryn trained her eyes up at Mia, and Mia instantly felt the force of her building climax.

"Laur—" Her chest heaved and she tried and failed to catch her breath. "Come here."

Lauryn pulled away, fingers still as she stood.

"No, no, no. Please don't stop." Mia grabbed her by the back of her neck and kissed her hard, Lauryn's lips slick with the taste of her.

Lauryn increased the pace of her thrusts again, mumbling against Mia's lips about how good she tasted, felt, how much she wanted Mia to come for her. The second she'd said it, Mia began to unravel in her hands. She whispered her name a hundred times, her body shaking all through it, fingers digging into Lauryn's back.

Lauryn held her until the aftershocks passed, one hand in a gentle caress on Mia's waist. And then she locked eyes with her and shook her head as if in awe. "I'm never going to get used to that, am I?"

Mia's laugh came out with the shaky consistency of not having enough air. "I sure hope not."

Lauryn pressed a kiss to Mia's clavicle before resting her forehead against her shoulder. "Happy Valentine's Day."

"Happy Valentine's Day, baby." Mia's lips grazed the lobe of Lauryn's ear, her hands moving to the clasp of Lauryn's bra. "That was really hot, but I need you in my bed now."

Lauryn grinned, taking Mia's hand to help her from the counter. "Thought you'd never ask."

EPILOGUE

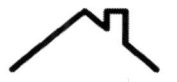

Lauryn blinked her eyes open and shifted slightly beneath the arm Mia had curled around her waist. Warmth emanated from Mia, despite the thin satin cami and shorts combo she slept in. Her lips hung slightly parted in the most endearing way, though Lauryn was sure Mia would deny ever sleeping with her mouth open. Six days. For six straight days, Lauryn had woken next to Mia, but today was the first time she'd done so in her new bed—her new *home*—and she couldn't explain the simultaneous peace and restlessness that had stirred her awake before nine on a Saturday morning. Last night, when they'd held each other close, talking well into the morning about what Mia's parents were like, and whether Lauryn was well and truly okay with meeting them tomorrow, she didn't know what to expect of the next morning. She'd slept in hundreds of places over her lifetime, but none of them really felt like hers; felt like home.

Her gaze roamed around the darkened bedroom, faint signs of daylight struggling to peek through the drapes. Darby had done an incredible job with everything from the theme of soft grays and silvers to the 18th century French vanity in the en suite. The elaborate chandelier hung over her bed was a bit much, but it complemented the rest of the room well.

Was this why she had come to Denver?

She glanced at Mia again and her heart swelled at the mere presence of her. After every trip to LA, New York, Miami, after every long day of guest appearances, interviews and performances, this was where Lauryn wanted to be. Maybe knowing Sully was what had led Lauryn here, but she knew she could never truly leave again.

Homes were as much people as they were places.

And Mia was home.

"I love you." Lauryn's whispered words settled in the stillness of the room and echoed in her mind.

Mia snuggled closer, burrowing her face between Lauryn's neck and shoulder. "I thought we agreed, no grand declarations on big days."

Somehow, even expecting her to be asleep, Lauryn didn't startle at Mia's voice, but simply pulled her closer, further intertwining their legs beneath the duvet. Lauryn probably wouldn't have picked this moment to say the words for the first time—at least half a dozen more curated settings had come to mind while just lying there—but this felt right. Not grand or elaborate. Simply words she'd spent too long trying not to say.

"You can't just go silent on me after that, you know."

Lauryn smiled, shifting to find beaming brown eyes trained up at her. "I didn't. You're just...impatient. As always."

"I just know what I want." She moved her hand across Lauryn's stomach, down Lauryn's right arm to interlace their fingers. Then, she tilted her chin up and pressed her lips to

Lauryn's in a chaste but lingering kiss. "I love you too, which is the only reason I'm kissing you when I've only barely opened my eyes."

Lauryn hummed. "Morning breath. The pinnacle of romantic gestures."

Mia laughed, and something swirled in Lauryn's belly—a feeling she never wanted to not experience ever again, that never failed to leave her in a haze of staring and smiling and wonder. Mia reached up and stroked her face. "I love you so much, Laur. I think I've been in love with you since the day we spent with Bella and Zac. I knew right then that you were everything I could ever want, and so much more."

Lauryn closed her eyes and released a slow breath. Relief washed over her. "It's so good to hear you say it."

"There was never any chance that I wouldn't."

"I know. Deep down, I think I knew you felt it, but I know after everything with—"

"Laur..." Mia propped herself up on one elbow, shaking her head slightly. "When I look at you, when I'm with you, when I think about you, all I see is *you*. I see you dressed for a blizzard on New Year's Eve, the way you looked at me that Monday when you walked into my office, all confused and concerned and maybe a little like you wanted to get me naked." She laughed and Lauryn couldn't help but join in. "I see boxes of sunshine, smell roses and vanilla, and I see someone my friends and family fell for as easily as I did. Anything before is another lifetime entirely."

Lauryn fell more in love with Mia every day, but today, cuddled up in a bed Lauryn hoped to call theirs instead of hers someday, she couldn't imagine falling any deeper. A smile tugged at her lips. "You know, you're kind of a romantic."

Mia playfully rolled her eyes. "Don't remind me. It's my solitary flaw."

"Solitary?" Lauryn teased.

"I don't like what you're suggesting."

"What I'm suggesting..." She gently pushed against Mia's shoulder, slipped one leg between her thighs, and pressed a kiss to her neck. "Is that you are as intensely beautiful as you are intensely driven, kind, loving and lovely." She pulled away to look Mia in the eyes again. "If you happen to have a flaw, or two, it wouldn't be that you're romantic and it wouldn't make you any less perfect. And I know all of this because I'm lucky enough to be loved by you."

Mia licked her lips, eyes locked on Lauryn's the whole way through. "Remind me to thank Drew later."

"Baby, one thanks is enough for a bottle of wine. Even an overpriced one."

She breathed a laugh, shaking her head as if Lauryn was completely ridiculous. "Not for the wine, Laur. For sending me you."

LAURYN PAUSED her strumming at the chime of the doorbell. She was two verses into a song with no name, but if the other three songs she'd written lately were any indication, her album would be entrenched in lyrics about loss and love. They weren't expecting any deliveries, or even caterers, with the housewarming party being close friends and family only, and it was too early for guests to start showing up already.

"Babe," Lauryn yelled toward the en suite attached to her bedroom. "I'm going to go get the door!"

"Okay, I'll be out in a second!" Mia called back.

Lauryn started toward the door, the carpet plush beneath the multicolored socks on her feet before shifting to the hardwood in the hallway. She breathed in the scent of fresh linen and pine, still acquainting herself with the splashes of vibrant colors among the generally neutral theme and rare instance of modern art.

The doorbell rang again as she opened the door to Darby and James with recyclable bags brimming with groceries.

"It's housewarming party day!" Darby beamed, stepping past Lauryn into the foyer.

"Hey, Laur." James bobbed her head in a subtle greeting, following as Lauryn closed the door behind them.

She spared a glance at the watch on her wrist. *10:17 a.m.* "Is it me, or are you guys like five hours early?"

"Oh no. I told you we'd come by early to help set up, remember?" Darby cocked her head slightly. "Yesterday, when we were texting about M's birt—"

"Hey, J and D."

Lauryn looked up at the sound of Mia's voice, and smiled at the sight of her—hair neatly swept up into a bun and face makeup free, dressed in one of Lauryn's hoodies and a pair of pink camo leggings. Mia's brows inched up at Lauryn's obvious ogling.

"We'll..." James trailed off, tugging Darby through an archway left of the foyer. "Be in the kitchen."

Lauryn snapped out of her daze. "Yeah. I'll just come show you where everything is."

"Oh no, we're good. Keep, you know—"

"Eye-fucking each other," James mumbled.

Mia laughed. "Back off, Jagerbomb. Let's see how many people you have eyes for when Zee shows up."

"Astrid and I are clearly the most well-adjusted couple.

But don't worry. We'll give you all tips on how to behave in front of company later." Darby disappeared through the living room with a bounce in her step, and a chuckling James beside her.

Lauryn stared after her in mild disbelief. "She's serious about those tips, isn't she?"

Mia nodded, grinning as she closed the gap between them and wrapped her arms around Lauryn's neck. "Completely."

"Thought so." She let her hands fall to Mia's hips, the fabric of her leggings smooth, curve of her ass tempting. "Yoga time?"

"Mhm. Although, I probably shouldn't leave you alone with those two."

"Darby said she'd be over early, but I thought maybe she meant like an hour or two early."

"Aw, baby, you'll learn."

"I'm sure I will." She punctuated her next words with a light spank. "Go do your workout. I have friend-in-laws to charm."

"Trust me. They're already charmed." She brushed a strand of hair out of Lauryn's face, her expression turning more thoughtful. "I know you really want to see Bella and Zac, but are you still okay with meeting my family?"

"I've already met Matt. He seems cool."

"Yeah. But now that he knows you're my girlfriend, he'll get all protective big brother, although he spent an hour interrogating me the day I told him, and he actually really likes you already. My mom will probably go on about how beautiful you are and ask a million questions about your music and your career—I told her your family is off-limits—"

"Mia..."

"Dad doesn't say much. He'll nurse one beer all night and watch everyone from a corner. Layla is really the most normal one."

"Baby." Lauryn squeezed her hips, pulling her closer. "I'm sure I'm going to love them. Sully and Angie, Blake and Drew will love you. It's a party with family. And as long as you're with me, I'll be fine."

"So, *it is* everything you wanted then? Somewhere that feels like the place family comes home to," Mia repeated.

"It is." Lauryn nodded, whispering the words onto Mia's lips. "In fact, I'd say it's pretty flippin' fantastic."

THANK YOU

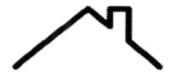

Thank you for reading COLLIDE. This was my first collaboration, and it feels so surreal that I got to do it with friends! Be sure to keep up with the rest of the Flippin' Fantastic trio by clicking the links below:

THE BRIGHT SIDE (DARBY)

AGAINST THE GRAIN (JAMES)

For updates on upcoming projects, sneak peeks and giveaways, subscribe to my newsletter or follow me on Twitter, Instagram or Facebook.

Remember to take breaks and be kind to yourselves.
— STEPH

KEEP READING

If you enjoyed *Collide*, keep reading for the first two chapters of my novel *Chef's Kiss*—a slow burn age gap romance between Valentina, a tenacious culinary school graduate and Jenn, the executive chef and owner of Mexican-Italian fusion restaurant Gia!

CHEF'S KISS

PREVIEW

STEPHANIE SHEA

chef's KISS

At least she had the job of her dreams, even if she could never have *her*.

SYNOPSIS

Valentina Rosas has always known what she wants. Mostly. Sort of. At least, she does now. And what she wants is the coveted staging role at Gia, San Francisco. With four years at the top of her class in culinary school and enough tenacity to fuel the entire Mission, no one doubts she is about to land the job of her dreams—including the three-person cheer squad made up of her best friend and adorably overbearing parents.

Renowned chef Jenn Coleman is not a people person. Her rise to the top of the culinary industry stems from a cultivated blend of top-tier schooling—from her nonna—and bouts of carefully managed misanthropy. Owning and operating two Michelin starred restaurants doesn't leave time for much else anyway. Just ask her ex.

When the new stage at her restaurant trips into her with all the grace of a baby giraffe, it's a sure recipe for disaster. But for all of Jenn's reserve, Valentina has twice the allure, and the chemistry between them is just...chef's kiss.

If only Jenn wasn't Valentina's boss with nearly ten years between them.

CHAPTER 1

Richmond, San Francisco, was a gorgeous place to die.

Valentina's heart raced, her lungs burning, feet quick against the paved trail as she upped her sprint through Golden Gate Park. The sun beamed across the sparsely cloudy sky, casting a glow over the evergreen shrubs and goldfields, and faint traces of lavender wafted in the air—always lavender, despite the medley of wildflowers scattered about the park. J Balvin echoed from her earphones at a reckless volume, drowning out the burble of the lake and chirp of birds she'd failed at identifying.

A pair of men darted by her in a blur of leopard print shorts. *Seriously?* The taller glanced back, shooting her a wink and a crooked smirk. If Val wasn't on her final mile and seconds from passing out, her competitive streak might've won out. But the Tai Chi group on the north lawn seemed that much more tempting.

Why had she decided to take up running again?

The words "stress relief" ricocheted in her mind in a voice that sounded suspiciously like Zoe's. Zoe, who was undoubtedly still asleep back at the apartment. A lifetime of friendship and Val still hadn't tapped into Zoe's level of Zen. Then again, it had been Val's idea to move an entire time zone and burn through her savings in one of the most expensive cities in the country, with its beautiful weather and varied terrain and art, and culture—*her* culture. And food. God, the food. Maybe moving was completely worth it even if she was verging on broke, and her dream was dead. She could almost hear her father's voice now, accent twice as heavy as the lilt in his tone. "You're a great chef, cariño, but your true calling is drama." Her lips curled up at the thought as she slowed her pace beneath the shade of a large oak tree and doubled over to grip her knees, catching her breath.

The beat of her music cut off, replaced by the insistent chime and buzzing of her phone. She cast a glance where it had been strapped to her left bicep, the screen lit up with an unidentified number. With as many job applications as she and Zoe had filled out lately, she did not have the luxury of letting her phone ring unanswered. Even if she would pick up sounding like a pack a day smoker. Then again, she couldn't remember ever getting a job offer on the weekend. "Hello?"

"Valentina Rosas de Leon?" The woman's tone carried the buoyancy of someone who spoke to people for a living, or at the very least, enjoyed it.

Val could relate—sort of—but the use of her full name meant one of two things. Offer or rejection. She forced down a gulp, trying to keep her tone even. "This is Valentina."

"Hi. I'm Avery, calling from Gia, San Francisco."

The pace of Val's heart picked up.

"Congratulations! You are this year's recipient of our

coveted staging post hosted by our very own Jenn Coleman."

Val blinked, her brows drawing closer, chest tightening. She mulled over the words in her mind, actually trying to pick out traces of Zoe's voice in the woman's tone. The staging spot for Gia had been announced. Three weeks ago. If ranting about it as recently as last night was any indication, Val had not made peace with losing something she'd dreamed of all through culinary school. But she wasn't delusional. And this was a prank too far. Even for Zoe. "Zo, if this is you—"

"This is Avery," the woman cut in gently, an audible smile in her voice.

Val paused, mumbling, "Avery," as if saying the name herself would somehow erase her confusion.

"Yes. From Gia. San Fran-cisco." She separated the syllables the way one did for a small child, and Val crossed her arms over her chest.

If this person was actually calling from Gia, she had very nearly ruined any prospect of making a positive first impression. But Avery was still on the phone, reiterating how Val had been picked for the staging position, and this made about as much sense as one ply toilet paper. She slid a hand across her sweat-dampened forehead, into her hair and down her ponytail. "I'm sorry. How is this happening?"

"What do you mean?"

"I mean, didn't the spot already go to that guy from Auguste Escoffier?" Tall, blonde, skipped too many leg days, looked like he could barely tell when oil was hot. Okay. Definitely not over it.

"Right," Avery chirped. "Unfortunately, he's no longer able to participate. Unforeseen circumstances and all that. But you, Valentina, come highly recommended by all your instructors at the Institute, and we would be so happy to have you if you're still open to joining us."

"Uh—Uhm. Yes. Of course." Was that even a real question?

Avery chuckled. "We understand this is unexpected and your plans for the summer may have changed. Would you be able to give us your answer in a day or two?"

How could she gracefully tell this woman that working at Gia was the plan of her life? "Yes." She shook her head. "I mean, thank you. I...don't need to think it over."

"Okay. I'm seeing here that you're in New York, but just so we're clear, you do know the summer staging role is for San Francisco, not Manhattan?"

"Yes. That won't be a problem. I actually moved recently."

"To San Francisco?" The question resounded with a skepticism that made Val balk.

"Yes?" Her answer was more than a little bashful.

"Wow. You are impressively prepared for this call."

Val could think of a few other ways to phrase moving to another state for a job she hadn't been offered, but there was nothing tying her to New York anymore. Besides, after a perfectly acceptable period of sulking, she'd convinced herself it was still possible. Okay, her parents and Zoe had convinced her. And sure, she'd have to do it the hard way—by waiting for an opening that met her qualifications, hoping her application caught their attention, then somehow impressing Jenn Coleman enough to be offered a spot in her kitchen. But here she was, running through a gorgeous park in San Francisco on the hinges of an audacious if ambitious plan, with Avery from Gia offering her the equivalent of an internship. Her favor with the universe was fickle as fuck, but days like this definitely made up for it.

"Well, we were slated to begin on the 6th, and while we are prepared to allow you an extra week, something tells me you're ready for that, too."

A laugh bubbled up in Val's chest, her breathing finally back to some semblance of normal. "The 6th works just fine."

"Be here at 10 a.m. I'll get you settled with some paperwork and give you a tour."

"Sounds perfect. Thank you, Avery."

"Looking forward to meeting you, Valentina."

The call ended with a beep and her thumb moved to cut off the booming resumption of "Loco Contigo" over her earphones. Her lips stretched in a smile as she replayed the conversation in her mind, wondering, *did that really just happen*? Across the lawn, the Tai Chi instructor had begun an awkward combination of bent knees and slow flailing arms that left him looking constipated, and Val's smile turned to a full-on laugh. When at least one participant in the front row—an older woman with striking silvery hair—shot her a disapproving glare, she turned toward the burbling lake and readied herself for a run back home. Zoe was never going to believe this.

VAL JOGGED up to the door of their building and keyed in the entrance code. It still amazed her that they'd managed to land an apartment in a recently constructed building that had all the new wave amenities of Virtual Doorman and Google Fiber Webpass, but no parking for her charmingly aged Prius. It made for its fair share of wrangling for nearby spots on the street, and each night, a routine glance out the window of their second-floor apartment before she could sleep, but what was the alternative? Trading the first meaningful thing she'd actually been able to buy herself for a bicycle she'd definitely wind up pushing up more hills than she cared to count?

Not. Fun.

Inside, she crossed the empty lobby, taking the stairs up to their apartment. Her body buzzed with excitement, and for the first time in the week since she'd started running again, she didn't feel on the verge of passing out at the door. As she unclasped her necklace to get to the key she wore as a pendant, she tried to remember if the lump beneath the blanket on Zoe's bed had looked big enough for two people to have been underneath when she'd left earlier this morning. Perks of sharing a place that had been advertised as a two bedroom, but actually turned out to be one with a second bed off to the far end of the living room. If Val had anticipated getting an eye full of some guy's remarkably manscaped junk a week into moving in, she would've thrown the deciding round of Rock, Paper, Scissors that had landed her the actual bedroom. It was her fault, really. She knew Zoe. Loved Zoe.

Zoe loved sex.

Sex with strangers? Even better.

Val pushed open the door with measured caution, one hand clasped tightly over her eyes. "I have news I'd prefer to share with everyone's clothes on."

Zoe's soft, infectious laugh filled the room. "Don't we have a standing promise to at least text if we have someone over?"

"Like you've never forgotten that promise." Val dropped her hand, grateful to find Zoe alone in a tank top and shorts as she straightened the corners of her comforter. She stood to her full height—a dignified five feet three with curves for days—and swept ruffled blonde curls out of her face.

"Okay, Val. Be a snarky bitch." She rolled her eyes—greyish blue orbs that always shone a little too brightly against her pale ivory skin. "So, I forgot once. Twice."

Val shot her a look.

"Maybe three times, but you're the one who brought home a screamer last week."

One of Val's brows inched up and she cocked her head to the right. "Fair." Of course, she had no way of knowing the woman would turn out to be so... expressive, but she did feel bad Zoe hadn't been able to sleep half the night. Especially since she'd had her first shift as a junior pastry chef at Cakes and Stuff the next day. A grin spread across Val's face at the memory of her call earlier, and she bent to start undoing her laces.

"Tell me you're not having flashbacks right now."

"What? No." She laughed, crossing their modest open floor plan to Zoe's "bedroom". "I got a staging offer."

"Really?" Zoe's eyes widened. "Where?"

"Gia."

Lines drew in her forehead. "How?"

"I don't even know, Zo." Val fell into the loveseat with no grace and too much drama, her smile never leaving her face. Could a person feel high on good news? Her memory's comparison to the few times she'd had pot brownies said yes. Absolutely. "The woman who called said the guy from Auguste had to drop out. I actually thought it was you for a second."

Zoe tsked, frowning. "I know my prank skills at the institute were A1, but I also know how badly you wanted that spot. I would never."

"I know." Val nodded. "I guess it just seemed so unbelievable." Somewhere, deep in her subconscious, there was a part of her that was disappointed to not have been the first pick—to have been offered the spot only because someone else could no longer take advantage—but she couldn't bring herself to dwell on it. It's not like she'd pass on the opportunity out of pride. She was a lot of things. Stupid wasn't one of them.

She gave Zoe a quick rundown of the details, knowing she'd have to go over them again when she called her parents. The look on their faces would be worth it though. Maybe they'd returned to Mexico having never quite attained the American dream, but she knew how much it meant to them to see her succeed. Even if it had taken an MBA she'd barely used and leaving a job with a comfortable salary to start all over at culinary school, then become essentially an intern at twenty-eight years old.

Zoe chuckled, shaking her head as she plopped down next to Val on the sofa. "Leave it to you to land exactly the job you wanted. I swear, I don't know if it's magic or sheer willpower."

"Probably both. Besides, it's not *exactly* the job I want."

"Right. Because your real plan is to walk into Gia, learn everything you can from Jenn Coleman and mutiny your way to head chef."

Val tossed her head back in a laugh. "I can't believe I'm two days away from standing in a kitchen with a living, breathing legend."

"A *gorgeous* living, breathing legend," Zoe enhanced.

Val shrugged, her gaze fixed on the lines of the ceiling. "Minor detail."

"Minor detail?"

"Mhm."

"I don't know, V." Amusement laced Zoe's exhale. "You

may swing both ways, but women like her are definitely your kryptonite."

Val sat upright and narrowed her eyes at Zoe's baby blues. "You have zero evidence to back that up."

Zoe's brows rose. "Our Intro to Gastronomy instructor?"

"Healthy admiration."

"You were ten minutes early everyday all semester."

"*And* an enthusiastic interest in my education."

"Sure."

"Even if you were right," Val acquiesced. Barely. "She was my instructor. I wouldn't have actually done anything about it. You know how badly I wanted Gia. Trust me." She stood to head to the bathroom for a shower. "I am not jeopardizing my chances of actually working there someday just because Jenn Coleman happens to have a nice face. Besides..." She glanced over her shoulder, actually thinking back to the screamer this time. Stevie, was it? "This city is full of beautiful people. I'm sure I'll do just fine."

CHAPTER 2

Gia, San Francisco, sat on the corner of Harrison Street, marked by a polished hanging wooden sign with the name in glorious swooping font. In the beaming glow of midmorning, it stood out like a beacon of hope—an aspiration come to fruition, built on blood, sweat, tears, and Jenn Coleman's genius take on Italian meets Mexican cuisine.

Val tightened her grip on the steering wheel of her third-hand Prius, angling her head to peer out the window at the building. Not that she had time for it. In fact, the digital clock on her dashboard screamed that she *really* didn't have time for it, but there was something enthralling if not intimidating about seeing the building up close; it's taupe horizontal siding and casement windows were the picture of simplistic. Maybe it was physically being there—this wasn't a rabbit hole Google search brought on by another fit of daydreaming. This was her opportunity to prove that finishing top of her class at the Culinary Institute of America was not a fluke, to charm these people with her talent and grace—okay, probably not grace per se, she was kind of clumsy sometimes—

Shit. Ten minutes before your first shift is not the time to be working through your imposter syndrome, Val.

A scarier thought entered her mind and she glanced down at her white button down. Had she put on deodorant? She tilted her head and chanced a sniff, almost immediately met by a subtle whiff of shea. Of course, she had.

Her phone buzzed in the holder fixed to her dashboard and the screen lit up with a text from her mom. Then another.

Mami (9:53 a.m.)
Buena suerte, mi vida.
Your father is planning a celebration for your first day.
Any reason to throw a party.

Val's grin exploded to a hearty laugh at the eye roll tacked onto the end of the message. When had her mom gotten so versed in emojis? Still, the presence of her, through a simple series of text, filled Val like the calmest of deep breaths, reminding her that belief in herself stemmed from an infallible support system, even with thousands of miles between them now. She gave herself a steadying look in the rearview mirror and made a mental note to reply to her mother later, when she had more time for the string of questions that would certainly ensue.

She grabbed her bag and exited her car onto the inclined sidewalk—not the steepest she'd encountered in the city so far—and crossed the few feet to Gia's main entrance. The scent of cheese and garlic hit the second she opened the door, and her eyes roamed the modest entryway. Ashwood floors, exposed beams and hanging lights. A simple layout of polished tables and chairs that read as modern rustic through daylight, but at night could easily pass as more elegant. Romantic, even. Although, the image her mind had recalled of the dim lighting and candle-lined wall ledges probably had everything to do with that. Unlike the well-stocked bar, the bread rack stood bare, and she found herself wondering if bakers were kneading away in the dough room right that second.

"Valentina?"

Her head snapped up at the sound of her name, the tap of heels more apparent at the sight of the woman approaching. She led with a smile that graced every inch of her delicate Asian features, dark hair caught in a ponytail that swung in her wake. "Avery?"

"Yes. Right on time." Her perfectly arched brows shifted in a way Val took to be approval.

"I'm just happy to be here."

"We're happy to have you." She gestured toward a four top then moved to slide one of the chairs back. "Sit, please."

Val took a settling gulp, sitting in the opposite chair. A sit down in the dining room two minutes after walking in wasn't what she'd been expecting. Nerves crept through her like tendrils on a vine. Interviews were a necessary evil. But were they? Wasn't the point of a stage that she wouldn't have to go through the nightmare of a personality test that usually went with a resume?

"Relax." Avery chuckled. "This isn't an interview. The stage is already yours. You're still required to do all your best work in the kitchen."

Val breathed a hopefully casual laugh. "HR and a mind reader."

"No. My brother just happens to be a chef, too. Aren't you all a bit anti-interview by default?"

"I feel like that's a trick question and I need to find a more diplomatic answer than yes."

Avery raised both hands. "No tricks here, I promise. But —" She glanced down at the gold classification folder in front of her and skipped over page one of, well, a lot. "There are a few things we need to go over before getting you into your whites. As you probably know, our staging process is more intricate and longer than most in the States, rounding out at four to six weeks. By the fourth, you'll know where you stand, if there's a chance of joining us on a more permanent basis, or trying elsewhere. Either way, a brief stint at a Michelin starred restaurant is usually enough to at least get our former stages in the door almost anywhere."

Didn't Val know it. But she didn't want just any starred restaurant. She wanted this one. She tempered the urge to blurt out as much, reaching for the small notepad and pen in her bag, listening intently as Avery went over salary, which, legal or not, didn't always come with a stage. Not that she minded either way. She'd budgeted this move down to the penny, and she had a six-sheet Excel doc to show for it. Pie charts included. Besides, she was confident that with enough drive and charisma—neither of which she'd ever been lacking—she could land a twelve-hour stage anywhere. Six weeks of hard work—zero delusions about that—for a chance at her dream seemed like a no brainer.

When Avery stood, announcing it was time for a tour, Val grabbed her notepad and followed with restrained zeal. At least, she hoped she'd managed a little restraint. Coming off as the eager, young intern was not the game plan. More of a seasoned newbie, one who'd seen enough of the world to know what she was about now. And, well, she'd seen New York, and Mexico City, which was close enough.

"I *will* let one of the kitchen staff take you through the actual tour of the kitchen since they are so much better at knowing where everything is, but in addition to the main dining room, we do have two private dining areas and a dough room. Guest bathrooms are on the first floor—we'll get to those in a bit—and the staff restroom is just off the break room in the back. There are two offices. One I share with Mel, our head chef, and Jenn's. Those are last on the trip. Questions?"

"How much time does she spend in there?" Val bobbed her head toward the kitchen. "Ms. Coleman, I mean."

Avery laughed, starting up a brief but winding flight of stairs, the spikes of her point toe pumps taunting in a way that made Val appreciate the pair of Chelsea boots on her own feet. "Code for how much opportunity will you have to learn from her?" Avery maintained her pace up the stairs without a glance back. "The answer to your question is a lot. We can't get her out of the kitchen, really. And don't call her Ms. Coleman. She hates it."

"Gossiping about me to our newest, Ave?"

Something tightened in Val's chest—exhilaration and panic bursting at its grip—and she paused a few steps beneath where Avery had gotten to the landing. Was that who she thought it was? Of course, it was. She could pick out the husk in Jenn Coleman's voice in a fifty-person choir. All those interviews. The one Iron Chef appearance Val had watched a questionable number of times. It was inspirational, engrossing. It was...

Jenn. Coleman.

She stepped into view, her hair swept up in a loose bun, skin soft and brown in the glow of morning light all around them, and Val was grateful she'd had the good sense to not utter Jenn's name out loud like a starstruck fan. *Jenn.* Something about it bounced around Val's mind with a distinct newness, which was weird because Val had probably mentioned her by name a few too many times in the last year alone. Had freckles always dusted her nose and cheeks like that?

"Is it even gossip if it's true?" Avery's retort punched a bit of sober into Val.

"I suppose not." Jenn leaned into the wrought iron of the small upstairs balcony, dazzling hazel eyes fixed on Val. "Welcome, Valentina."

Val's stomach flipped. Jenn Coleman knew her name, and she was officially what Zoe would lovingly term a basic bitch. "Hi, Miss—I mean, Jenn." She managed a smile. Barely. "I can't thank you enough for offering me this opportunity."

The closed lip smile Jenn returned seemed forced, awkward at best, though it gave away faint signs of a pair of dimples in her cheeks. She started toward the landing of the stairs, and Val resumed her ascent, bracing herself for a terse handshake and minimal eye contact. This didn't seem like part of the plan—running into their boss midtour. She anticipated quick and painless. She anticipated Jenn disappearing after, finishing her tour with Avery then changing into her whites and getting set up in the kitchen. Twelve hours on her feet would be hard, but she'd anticipated that too, even splurged on a pair of dreadful Birkenstock Londons. She did *not* anticipate tripping on the final step, or the embarrassing squeal that had wrenched its way from the back of her throat.

The pair of hands on her—one on her arm, the other firm on her waist—registered before the fact that she'd closed her eyes. She opened them to a delicate three chain necklace nestled against warm brown skin, gold circular pendant between the open top buttons of a simple black button down. *Shit*. Her gaze snapped up to Jenn's—a kaleidoscope of forests and fire staring back at her—and every rationale said her chest would give under the violent race of her heart. But she *had* almost crashed to the floor in front of her boss on day one. Would the fall have killed her? Unlikely. The embarrassment? Jury's still out.

"Oh my gosh. Are you okay?"

Val shrunk back at the alarm in Avery's voice. "Jesus. I'm so sorry. I'm clumsy on my feet, but great with my hands, I swear."

Jenn's brows crept up and her eyes widened ever so slightly.

"I mean—" Val cleared her throat. This was what she'd brought to the table—terrible coordination and a ruthless case of foot in mouth. *Nice, Valentina.*

"We understand." Jenn straightened, posture nearly as rigid as the lines of her lips. Clearly, Val was not making a good impression. And yet, she couldn't help thinking from her vantage point—close enough for the scent of shea and chamomile to dominate the permanence of spices and cheese in the air—pictures, videos... They really didn't do Jenn justice. She took a step back then moved to walk around where Val now stood safely on the landing. "I'll let you get back to your tour, Ave. Valentina."

Val didn't know what to make of the way Jenn had said her name. All politely dismissive. She willed her head not to turn when Jenn's shoulder brushed hers, to follow with her eyes as Jenn disappeared down the stairs.

Avery's eyes lit up with mischief and a grin spread on her face. "Way to make an impression."

Maybe it was the teasing quality of her tone, or her earlier assertion that nothing leading up to Val's duties in the kitchen had any bearing on her staging at Gia, but she felt comfortable enough to shut her eyes and breathe a laugh. Even having just experienced the third most embarrassing moment in her life. "She hates me."

"No." Avery chuckled. "She can come off as being a little

stoic, but Jenn doesn't hate anyone. Once you get in the kitchen and get to know her a little better, you'll see."

Suddenly, the concept of facing Jenn in the kitchen seemed more daunting than anything. How would Val erase the ineptitude of what had just happened? Had Jenn noticed that Val, however briefly and completely unconsciously, had stared at her chest? Did she now think Val was some kind of sleaze? *Ugh*. And the hands. Why the fuck would she say the thing about the hands?

"Come on," Avery beckoned. "I'll take you through private dining and I can't give you names, but I can tell you stories about worse first encounters with our other stages. Starting with the guy who mumbled 'I love you,' on his first handshake with Jenn then proceeded to fake a fainting spell."

Val's jaw dropped, disbelief and amusement all twisted into her expression. The tension in her body began to lift. The last five minutes were still stuck on loop in her head, but she appreciated what Avery was trying to do. When the time came, she'd just have to leave it all in the kitchen—let her skill and the talent she'd spent the last four years honing speak for themselves—and hope that it was enough.

ALSO BY STEPHANIE SHEA

Whispering Oaks: a wlw romantic suspense

Liquid Courage

Avalanche: a queer romance novelette

Apt 103: a queer romance short story

The Gia, San Francisco Romance Series:

Chef's Kiss

Missed Connection

ABOUT THE AUTHOR

Stephanie Shea is a self-proclaimed introvert, who spent her days in corporate daydreaming of becoming a full-time novelist.

Her favorite things include binging tv shows, creating worlds where no character is too queer, broken or sensitive, and snacks. Lots of snacks.

Someday, she hopes to curb her road rage, and get past her anxiety over social media and author bios.

stephaniesheawrites.com